BLOOD
DONORS

BLOOD DONORS

STEVE TASANE

WALKER
BOOKS

First published in Great Britain 2013 by Walker Books Ltd
87 Vauxhall Walk, London SE11 5HJ

10 9 8 7 6 5 4 3 2 1

This book has been typeset in ITC American Typewriter

Printed and bound in Great Britain

British Library Cataloguing in Publication Data: a catalogue
record for this book is available from the British Library

ISBN 978-1-4063-4405-9

www.walker.co.uk

For Tim

Anger Management Issues

Monday mornin' first lesson <u>a bedbug crawls right outta my ear and down my neck</u>.

I'm already sore at my boy Mustaph 'cos he don't ever do nothin' but sleep, see? I think he sufferin' from bein' sad, 'cos he spend half his life in bed, and it all wrong 'cos we be fifteen which is the primetime, yeah? We be hittin' on girls and playin' our beats and footie and crazy stuff on computer, but only if ol' Mustaph can drag his dozy head out from under his duvet – that boy win Olympic Gold for sleepin'.

Nine o'clock I call at his on my way out of the block. We live on different floors on The Finger. The Finger is one big tower block, only one for miles around. Where most of my boys live, and my mum and my aunties and their boyfriends. Anyone who anyone to anyone, all livin' in The Finger. As if they scoop up the flats from a normal estate and pile them up high like a game of Jenga, all wobbly and jagged. Somehow The Finger stay up, all twenty floors of it. Mum says it's all us in The Finger, stickin' up against the rest of the world.

Anyways, Mustaph's place is a few floors below

mine and I always knock on my way down. If he's
awake we hang together.

Monday mornin', this boy ain't risin' for nobody,
so first lesson he be marked absent and I'm sittin'
next to this fool Ashley, who thinkin' he my <u>friend</u> on
account of bein' into hip hop stuff I was into when
I was still in Year 5, get me? I'm cool with it, but
Ashley be always in my face.

Monday mornin' ain't no exception. So what
happen? Borin' old Subo the maths teacher is dronin'
on about hippopotamus triangles and Ashley turn
to me, pullin' some dumb face and <u>a bedbug crawls
right outta my ear and down my neck</u>.

Earlier that mornin', I'd woken up itchin' like
a bitch.

Mum yells me out for usin' language, yeah, but
I tell no lie. I was itchin' like a bitch. I counted the
bumps on my leg. Just countin' on my left leg for
sure, but them badassed bumps coverin' every inch
of my skin. I counted up to twenty-eight and then I
submitted. Them li'l bugs must have sucked three
pints of blood. How thirsty is that? I'm thinkin' I'm
gettin' paler and paler every day. Any day now I wake
up, find I turned into the ghost of myself.

I cussed out loud and threw the duvet off of me
and squinted down at the bed sheet. I was seein'
about a dozen of them bugs scatterin' like a gang
after a slumpin'. Only it's me, Marshall O'Connor the
First, that'd been slumped, and I wasn't standin' for

it. I slipped into my boxers and bust into the kitchen. Mum's sittin' there readin' a letter and I blatted it outta her hands and start cussin' straight away.

Not the perfect start to the week, I admit. But these bedbugs been gettin' worse and worse as we sweatin' through blazin' hot summer. Heatwave showin' no sign of coolin' even now, second week back at school.

Mum tried to play it down first off, callin' them creepy-crawlies as if I'm still in little school like my bro Connor – that's Connor O'Connor the First, yeah, don't ask – and we on some infant visit to the zoo. But it ain't no zoo, it's mine and Connor's room, and it ain't right. It proper nasty.

Oh, look, it's one of them creepy-crawlies. She flick it away like it was a ant or a ladybird or a incy wincy spider crawled up the spout.

After a while, I'm sayin' *Hey, Mum, there's another bug.*

Bugs I started callin' 'em, 'cos bugs is what they are.

When I blatted the letter out her hand, Mum leap to her feet, snatch up the letter, shove it in her pocket, and shoot me her look. Her look is fierce. I'm bigger than her but she must have invisible muscles in her eyeballs 'cos she feed me the look and it's like I been slapped round the face. She cussed me out, sayin' how she told me about usin' language like that and if I wanna use them kind of words she'd give me proper reason to cuss big time.

Then she surprised me by turnin' her back. I hate it when she does that. Like I disgust her, she can't bear the sight of me. With her back to me she tell me I'm already late and I make her shamed. Nex' thing I know I'm outta the door only half dressed and stuffin' books into my school backpack like I am a unprepared fool. *Aren't things bad enough?* she cries. *See how you make things worse!* Door slams shut and I'm guessin' that's me on the way to school. Nice start, yeah?

Get what I deserve.

I shoulda risen early like my kid brother, and bypassed the battlin' business. Connor got this obsession with arrivin' at his school before anybody else, so he can stand all alone in the playground and pretend he in a movie where it's the end of the world and he's the only human left alive. My brother a bit weird.

I never seen Mum this bad before. We always used to have a blast, me and her and li'l Con-Con rollin' roun' havin' hysterics playin' chase and catch with my mutt Sabretooth.

All the time I was walkin' I was scratchin' my itches, thinkin' Just imagine how it'd be, if word got out about this at school. Man, I'd be dead meat.

So here we are, in class, surrounded by all my boys, a handful of enemies and way too many girls to have a humiliation heap itself on top of me. It's like I got predicative skills like Derren Brown. I predic' big bad bug trouble.

Moment that bedbug crawl outta my ear gonna last for ever in my life. I see Ashley's jaw drop in disgust same time as I feel that bug's legs ticklin' against my skin. I slap my neck and squish it dead. Its blood – _my_ blood – is smeared across my palm. Me and Ashley are just starin' at it, and Ashley mutters _Whoa, man, you infested!_ What am I supposed to do?

I bunch my fist and I smash his face. Blood squirts outta his nose same as my blood squirted outta the bug. He topple over his chair and nex' thing I know I'm on top of him, poundin' the life outta him. Subo got his arms tucked under my pits, tryin' to drag me off and he's yellin _O'Connor! O'Connor!_ and callin' one of the other kids to go get help. Ashley is a bloody mess. Subo pulls me up and I'm yellin' _You filthy, filthy, you dirty, nasty, filth_ and I'm pointin' at him and lookin' at the rest of the class as if it be Ashley had the bug crawlin' outta his ear and needs disinfectin' and nobody oughta go near him in case they gonna get his germs. I'm cussin' his filth as other teachers come in and drag me out.

It all Mustaph's fault, 'cos if he wasn't no sleepy bones it's him would be sittin' next to me in class and I wouldn't have to bash that fool Ashley, would I?

All I can think is It's not fair, it's not fair as I'm dragged to the Head, and I've got a suspension. Again. They say I got anger management issues. My mum says I got it off of my dad.

Mum. She gonna go ape.

Biff

I trudge home thinkin' how Mum goin' to think I
let us down again. *See how you make things worse*
she'd said. But none of it would have happened if it
hadn't been for the bug crawlin' out my ear. And it's
on account of the bugs we battled each other before I
went to school. Now we goin' to battle some more.

Sun is shinin' but it feel like rain is fallin'.

I walk up the stairs to our place on the tenth floor,
a condemned man steppin' up to the judge. *Mum?* I
say when I come through the door. *Mum?*

I forgot. She's out, doin' her cleanin' job. So I got
to stress all the rest of the day, waitin' to face my
sentencin'.

I whistle my dog. Least he's pleased to see me,
jumpin' up, lickin' my face, whinin' and waggin' his
tail like a helicopter-dog. Sabretooth is cross-breed,
a mongrel like me. I was watchin' this programme
on TV with a vet sayin' how cross-breeds are
the fittest dogs 'cos they got all the best bits of
different breeds, but none of the worst bits. I'm
thinkin' that's me. I got Irish and I got Jamaican

and Mum say I even got a little Canadian too, which make me fitter and healthier than every other boy. Connor's dad was Italian. That means I <u>gotta</u> be fitter than him. Mum says no, it's all the same mix, if we was a PIE chart we'd be sliced up the same, but with different nationalities. I'm tougher than Con-Con but he's a few years younger than me yet. I wonder if my dad ever faced up to Connor's dad, which would win in a scrap?

But we ain't never seen Connor's dad, and mine I ain't seen since back in the day. Way back. Whatever, my dad would bash Connor's dad – easy.

Talking like that Mum says, *is why you're always in trouble at school.*

Even when she's not home, I got her voice condemnin' my ears.

Stroke Sabre. My dog ain't never met my dad. If he did I'm sure he'd lick his face. Sabre lick every face. He that kind of dog, everybody's pal. My social worker says he's a <u>calming influence</u>. True. Sabretooth my mutt, what Mum got me for my eleventh and is now my closest and most trusted.

Even when I get you a puppy, you still come home with another boy's blood on your shirt.

Irritatin', like a ancient ringtone, shoulda been updated way back.

I pick up Sabre's favourite ball and his lead, which we never really need on account of him bein' so close and loyal, which is what make him as good a friend as Mustapha – he even sleep about the same as that boy – and we race up a couple of floors and drop in on Sis, see if she's wantin' to go stroll.

Share with her, about the bugs, and all.

I ain't stressed about showin' my face to Sis. Sis is my best friend next to Mustapha and Sabre, 'cept she older than me, don' go to school no more. Permanently excluded, yeah? Sixteen and not really my sis by blood, like Connor is my brother by blood, my half-brother. Sis is a mate, and though my social worker might not agree, my mum and everybody else praise her as a calming influence on me too. If she was my real sis I couldn't have done better. She never be sore and cussin' or punchin' nor nothin'. She jus' got a wicked smile, like seein' the joke in everythin'. Personally, I don' know what so funny.

Sis is the only person I know who ever got sent outta school for laughin'. She jus' used to sit in lessons and laugh at dates and figures and poems until it drove them teachers nuts. In the end they kicked her right out. She laughed all the way through them school gates. Sometimes, when I'm with her and idiots make me ready to explode she jus' look at me and grins and all my red rage lifts and I can't help but grin back. Nex' thing we know, it's twenty minutes later and I ain't hit nobody. Truly, I got the bes' things in the world to stop me blowin' my lid: Sis smilin' at me, Sabreboy lickin' my face, and ol' sleepyhead Mustaph, whose only real exercise is yawnin' his big hippo mouth.

I got the worst too. How comes we the only family in the whole block got bedbugs declarin' squatters' rights in our livin' room? How'm I gonna deal with them? Mum certainly ain't liftin' no finger. Con-Con too young. Won't be long now before word breaks out, spreads round The Finger. Nex' thing we know we be treated like we got Plague at our door. Ain't nobody goin' to want to know us.

Ain't nothin' for it. I got to spill it all to Sis. She is safe.

Sis can see I'm in a state, fixes me nice cool juice. We drink it standin' at her balcony lookin' down on the surroundin' estates. People roun' these parts say The Finger is where the council puts all what they call <u>antisociable families</u>. Sure, we got enough music bangin' out here and there, but Sis says that be a party somewhere to go to, and it don' cost no money for travel up West End and drinks and stuff. Course, me and Con-Con ain't invited to no grown-up parties. But we pals with this family in the flat under ours and they got the maddest widescreen you ever seen, and Sis know someone can get the latest movies and Mum make gigantic pots of popcorn. We draw the curtains with about a dozen of us all squashed in and we see brand-new films and we ain't spent a penny. So what's <u>antisociable</u> about that?

Bugs. Bugs is antisociable. Me and Con ain't goin' to get invited to no more popcorn parties if we smuggle in stinkin' gate-crashers.

Me and Sis look down at all the other estates. We got the baddest view and we all look out for each other and the magic is, you can <u>see</u> when people come visitin' that we don't want visitin', 'cos they park down there and word gets up – bailiffs, benefits inspectors, all of them.

We standin' there twelve storeys up, and Sabretooth has his paws up, poking his nose over the edge at grey clouds, heavy with attitude. Maybe the hot weather finally goin' to break. Sis clamber up onto the top of the wall and stand tall, stretchin' her arms out into the breeze, like she Queen of the City. Her hair blowin' and her smile beamin' sunshine. She's hundreds of feet up and she rules.

You're crazy I'm sayin'.

This the best feelin' ever she grins. *Y'oughta try it, Marsh.*

Sure, when I ain't got no reason for livin' no more. Then maybe I'll go for a dive. Right now, I'm good and safe down here.

She let free a sigh of satisfaction and take a deep intake of high-rise air. No traffic fumes up here, yeah? *This is my mountaintop* she says.

You keep a secret, Sis?

No she says, dead sarcastic. *I'll tweet it, Facebook it and text everybody I know*. She waggles her fingers together, hops off the wall onto the balcony. *Gimme gimme.*

So back inside I tell her I been suspended again. She laugh long and loud and say I'm gonna end up jus' like her.

Tell her about the bugs, I'm thinkin', *tell her about the bugs.*

Mum is goin' to hit the roof I say.

Sis shrugs. *She'll bounce back down, land on the carpet, nice and soft, soon enough.*

Tell her about the bugs.

No time at all Sis continue, *she'll be makin' you fresh popcorn.*

Yeah, make me feel really guilty.

Sis puts up her fists like a boxer. *You rather have a mum who slap you roun' the face?*

It'd be simpler I frown. *She settin' me all these good examples, I still come home suspended, batter some boy.*

Why don't I tell her about the bugs? I can't. I jus' can't. She gonna think I'm filth. Who I gonna have left then? Mustaph and Sabretooth. Woo hoo.

A year ago, Mum call in council pest control and a crew in boilersuits and gas masks with canisters on their backs and tubes attached to rubber pipin', like they was extras in *Dr Who*, yeah – came and fumigated the whole place. Like we was full of germs, needed sterilization. Connor and Sabe was following them fumigators roun' like it was the best thing since canned sandwiches, but me and Mum was lookin' down from our balcony, seein' the van parked beneath with PEST CONTROL tagged on the side in big pink letters. We knew everybody else in The Finger'd be peerin' down also. Everybody gonna know that it be us, the O'Connors, in need of emergency fumigation.

Mum must have figured it was worth the shame, to be free of the bugs crawlin' all over our walls, suckin' our arms and legs while we slept.

But no. They came back, didn't they? Came back with a vengeance. So now it so bad Mum turnin' her back on me, she so stressed and shamed.

Sis chuck me some crisps, which I'm sharin' with my mutt. And I spot one of them bugs crawlin' up her livin' room wall. Sabretooth must've scratched it off of his belly. Here it is creepin' its way straight towards a photo pinned on the wall. Plannin' on movin' in. It been usin' my dog as a Bug Bus. It goin' to hide behind the picture, wait until nightfall. Bitin' time.

That's what they do, see? Durin' daytime they hide and sleep off their feasts. I used to have this big poster of Ashley Young. One day me and Con-Con was havin' a row about our space, 'cos we each got a bed against opposite walls, meanin' the middle bit is shared territory. Little bruv who ain't no Man United fan was makin' big stress about my Ashley Young, pride of place, middle of the middle bit. So I goes to move it. I pull out the drawin' pins, pull the poster away from the wall and there's a riot of bugs all runnin' for cover, and in the corners there's dozens of little black full stops – which is bug poo – all over it. I screwed up my poster 'cos it was ruined. I was so mad I went over to Con-Con's poster of Iron Man and I rub my hands all over it, hard as I can, squish all of them bugs behind it. I could feel 'em splattin'. *I'm gonna execute you!* Con yelled, and he punched me between my legs, which hurt worse than any other way you can be hurt. I had to put him in a bear hug till he calmed down. When we peeled the poster off the wall, it was blood carnage, squished bedbugs all over.

So here comes another, plannin' on makin' a meal of Sis. I'm wantin' to squish it, but I'm stressin' about Sis seein' and knowin' what we bringin' into her home. I dunno where to look, or what to do.

I'm a rat, carryin' disease from neighbour to neighbour.

<u>Biff.</u> Sis squashes it flat with her bare hands. *Bye bye, little fella* she sings, wipin' her hand on her jeans. She sniffs her hand. *Poo, those things stink.*

I'm sittin' frozen, not knowin' what to say.

Sorry 'bout that she says. *These've been gettin' worse and worse for months. D'you get 'em in your place too?*

It feel like a cool rain a-fallin', after months of blisterin' heat.

Soft Stuart

I can remember a summertime in my life that
was jus' laughter and play, before bug bites and
stinkin' bins and hot-head fights. Before Con-Con,
when it was jus' me and Mum and Dad. I must've
been five, six, just a baby. Dad rented a big flat with
huge rooms, ceilin's high as the sky, and places for
hide-and-seek and chase, and big bouncy sofas and
proper beds and what they call a dinin' room. The
dinin' room had a wooden table big as a stage. Dad
used to lift me onto it and peoples gather roun' and
I'd do the Moonwalk. Everyone whistle and whoop.
Dad'd lift me on his shoulders and parade me roun'
to all the cheerin'. My head still didn't reach the
ceilin' because our house back in the day was bigger
even than a castle.

That's what we called it, The Castle. Mum and Dad
was the King and Queen.

Mum and Dad used to give parties. Everybody
come from miles around and play music and dance
and be drunk, Mum and Dad leanin' into each other,
laughin' together. Like they needed each other to stop

themselves fallin' over, on account of life bein' too funny to stay standin' straight. I had a zillion toys. Every toy I jus' snap my fingers 'cos I was Prince Marshall O'Connor the First. My mum and dad was rulers of the whole wide world.

Dad used to run his own business, successful, so successful he able to spare time with us at home. Mum used to do part-time nursin'. Dad said she didn't need to do that, but Mum said she enjoyed it. Helpin' people. Mum always been like that.

But that was a different world, back in the day. I remember how jus' before he lef', everythin' gone nasty. He be smashin' everythin', and the police invaded our Castle and Dad punchin' them all but they was more than him. The police punched him back, and they took him. All of a sudden he wasn't King, but Fighter.

Mum say I get my temper from him, inherited it like fortune. All them other riches jus' fell away.

Me and Mum moved into The Finger. Finger wasn't so bad in them days. Lift worked and there wasn't bad smells. I hated it jus' the same. Mum'd sit around, lookin' empty, like life had slipped out of her. I suppose I sat roun' pretty much the same way. They put Dad in prison, but The Finger, to me, was a prison also. I don't mean little bare rooms with cracks in the walls and no carpets and echoey corridors. That ain't where it's at. I understand prison. Prison is where Dad can't be with me and Mum. Prison is where me and Mum can't be with Dad. Same place.

He never came back, did he? Never so much as wrote. What happened to all his promises?

Nearest we get to royalty now is Sis and Big Auntie. I can't believe they got bug trouble too. I'm sittin', open-mouth, Sabreboy huddled between my legs, rufflin' the fur round his neck. I say to Sis *What, what? You telling me you got a infestation also?*

Infestation. That word I learned about when you got more bugs than you can count. Like these bloodsuckers come into our territory and attack us, like the police came and battled Dad, which was why everythin' turn dark. Now, even though we ain't got much space here in The Finger, these bugs comin' and infestin' us anyway. It ain't right. Why ain't they goin' marchin' on the big mansion houses? They get richer pickin's there. Nicer wallpaper to drop their full-stop poos.

Yahh Sis waves a hand dismissively. *You get used to it, innit. Communal livin', yeah? People downstairs got bedbugs, we got bedbugs, people upstairs got bedbugs. They creep through the cracks, yeah? We wanna be glad we ain't got no cockroaches, 'cos that bad, boy, I'm tellin' you.*

Always on the bright side, that's Sis.

Right there and then we hear sirens nee-nawin' up from the street below, and rush back to the balcony to see what goin' down.

An ambulance, pullin' up right outside the entrance to The Finger. We see a crew runnin' out carryin' medical bags and a rolled-up stretcher.

Some sad person had another bad accident says Sis.

All summer we gettin' meat wagons visitin' us here in the tower block, 'cos right here citizens always managin' to do a hurt to themselves, or each other. Sometimes it jus' families, mums and dads battlin' each other. Other times it be knife fights, someone gettin' shanked, which is dumb. I mean why you wanna go and stab some boy from your own estate? They jus' as likely to go and stab you back. Then you both be bleedin' and dyin' in your mama's arms. Don' make no sense. Sometimes it's drugs, which don' make no sense either. Why people wanna injec' themselves with stuff that poison them dead?

People do it 'cos the rest of their crew do it.

My dad used to say *If your best friend jump off the edge of a cliff, you go follow him, what that make you?*

He give me that serious look, straight in my eyes like a laser.

Tell me I said.

It make you a lemon.

And I ain't no lemon.

Dad never followed no gangs, had no need, he was one-man gang. Didn't do no drugs neither. Always said that me and Mum got him as high as he needed

to go. *Ain't no better buzz than the love of my leadin'
lady* he said, *nor my Little Prince.*

That was me: Little Prince.

When I was titchy, Dad was always tellin' me things,
sharin' sayin's, makin' cracks about life. Mum says I
got my temper from him. But that ain't right. I got his
wisdom. That's why I'm my own man. The only gang I
need is my family, and Mus, and Sis, and my dog.

I remember three times, people goin' and doin'
suicide, which make even less sense – slittin'
themselves like they jus' want their life to flow right
outta them, drip, drip down the drain. Worse, a year
ago, someone jump. Jump from the top floor, dive
straight off of the balcony – splat. Mum saw it with
her own eyes, but she say I don' wanna look. I'm
thinkin' she tellin' the truth, 'cos bad business is
down on the concrete below. Lemon Squash.

Ain't no authority gonna come and do nothin'
about all this. Far as they concerned we all just a
bunch of scuzzies. Get what we deserve.

Now the <u>nee-nawin'</u> is back. We listen out. We can
hear the ambulance men huffin' and puffin' up the
stairs on account of the lift not workin' which keeps
us all fit and seein' what happenin' on all the other
floors.

Sis always keep her door open, so's her family can
take in visitors without havin' to stretch themselves
up from the sofa. Theirs is a Open House. Any peoples
can drop in, like a public library. Big Auntie full of

knowledge. It safe, 'cos nobody goin' to bring trouble through their door. Big Auntie got respect. Sis mus' have about a dozen other brothers like me up and down The Finger. Her mum – Big Auntie – is like who everybody gonna turn to when they got a problem need fixin', or they got disagreement with one another and in need of a refereein' voice, 'cos no one gonna argue with Big Auntie. She's block warden – not the official one put down on the groun' floor by the council, who never here anyway – but the warden as chosen by the citizens livin' here, get me? Sis keep an eye on the younger ones, which is why everybody know her as Sis.

These meat men huff and puff right past Sis's door and up the nex' flight. We crane our necks 'cos we hear them bangin' and crashin' in the flat right above. We can hear a woman wailin' and screechin' and the meat men are yellin' 'structions. Big panic.

Sis meet my eye. *Soft Stuart* she say. *He does drugs. Hard stuff.*

She tilts her head at me and walks towards the door. She means we got to go and take a peek. Sis's mum ain't in, and she gonna wanna know what's happenin'. So she know what to tell peoples later on.

We tiptoe up the stairs. I ain't sure I want to go. I'm afraid we goin' to see a dead person. I don' know Soft Stuart. I don' wanna know Soft Stuart. I certainly don' wanna see no Soft Stuart body bein' carried out, face covered by a blanket like on some cop show on

TV. But I follow Sis 'cos that what I gotta do. I wanna reach out and hold her hand. Cuss myself for bein' a baby. I'm fifteen, yeah?

We get to Soft Stuart's flat. The door is open where the medic people barged in. Smell waftin' out worse than any I smelled before, mix of bedbugs and sweat and fear.

I wanna ask Sis if whole block crawlin' with bugs, but she put a finger to her lip – *shush*. Leans her head through the doorframe. Behind her, I crane my neck, take a look. I see the first body I ever seen in my life.

Soft Stuart is slumped on his sofa. He's as skinny as a street lamp and as white as a sheet. The three meat men are crouched round him, shakin' their heads like 'tain't no use, this man is mos' definite dead. Oh, he is white. I don' mean he is white like Connor is white. He is white like a sheet of paper. That is wrong, ain't nobody white like that, not dead nor alive. He's as white as a ghost that seen a ghost. He got a puncture in his skinny white arm. His eyes are wide open like he realized at the last moment that he gonna die. But too late, 'cos death already bitten him in the arm.

Drugs Sis silently mouths to me. *Oh dear.*

She shakin' her head, like she expectin' this kind of thing if people gonna mess with the bad stuff. *Oh dear* she say again.

I cuss myself for a fool. She ain't mouthin' <u>Oh dear</u> at all. She sayin' <u>OD</u>. Overdose.

I'm sweatin', ain't I?

One of the medics mutters *Open and shut case*, like someone open up a case and take a look, see what's in it and lock it shut again, on account of the contents bein' clearly not what you wanna take outta the case. A girl standin' over them that I seen aroun' the block, with her fists bunched up to her face. Mus' be Soft Stuart's girlfrien', sobbin' and gaspin' like she run out of breath. Grievin'.

Soft Stuart glares at me. His eyes are clean poppin' out of his head, screechin' *Oh my God! Oh my God! Oh my God!*

I thought overdosin' on heroin made you nod out, fall asleep, fade out of life. Don' make no sense. Soft Stuart look more like he was tortured to death. His mouth a rictus gape, like he died screamin'.

One of the meat men frowns at me, look of disgust, like he think I'm part of this scene.

Sabretooth whines. I look down and see he done a little accident, tricklin' along the floor.

A shiver runnin' through me. *Come on* I whisper to Sis, *let's go.*

Beatin' Up the Tree

Me and Sis watch from her balcony as they take Soft
Stuart away. 'Zackly as I thought, on a stretcher with
a blanket coverin' him from his ankles up over his
head. His toes stickin' out, like his feet are wantin'
to walk him back to life. His girl sobbin' and wailin'
behind him, like if she screeches enough it'll help his
toes get twitchin' again. Small crowd of rubberneckers
gathered roun', takin' pics to share with their mates.
Sick. Sis is bangin' on about how drugs is spoilin' the
block and it is time people oughta be takin' a stand.

Meat wagon drive off, but ain't no sirens blarin'
this time. *Ain't no need of 'em, now* says Sis. But she
don't say nothin' about no terror writ all across Soft
Stuart's face. Maybe I imagined it.

Didn't imagine no dead body though, did I?

So here I am, two minutes later, bangin' on Mustaph's
door. *Come on, fool! Let me in. I got stuff to tell. Oi!
Mustaph! Hey, man! Wake up!*

Soft Stuart's eyes are still fixed on me, like the
blazin' sun when you glare directly at it – still there

even when you shut your eyes tight. Burnt into your vision.

I knock and knock so I almost make a fist-shaped hole in the door. You always got to knock at Mustaph's door 'cos he the only fool in the whole postcode ain't got no mobile phone. Sis got him one once, for free, no cost, so he could hardly say no, could he? I'm callin' him a day later and he ain't answerin' so when I see him I say *Where's your mobile, man?*

He say *Oh, I left it somewhere.*

Where? Where you left it?

Dunno. And that was that.

Finally I hear a shuffle shuffle and a *Yeah, yeah,* the click and clunk of deadlocks and bolts and chains all bein' undone. Door opens a crack.

Mustaph's dad tilts his chin up at me and turns away, strollin' through to their livin' room, where all of Mustaph's sisters are squeezed together on the sofa, eatin' sweets, glued to the TV. I veer left into Mustaph's den.

Mus always in the darkness, curtains drawn, light bulbs unscrewed. My boy live by candlelight and torch beam. When you walk in his place you never know whether he there, not there, dead, alive, sleepin' or disguisin' himself as some bad art experiment. He got a full-size human skeleton hangin' down from the ceilin', dressed in a bright orange boilersuit, and a bust of Beethoven's head on a chest of drawers next to a life-size crow. Everythin' plastic, but lookin' real enough to make you wonder whether the boy actually sane. He keep a impressive collection of dolls as well. Spray-painted and amputated and in some cases operated on so they got too many limbs or inappropriate heads. Every inch of wall, ceilin', floor sprayed with swirlin' colour and shape. I mean, who could sleep at all in here, never mind sleep the eighteen hours a day Mustaph seem to?

Any fool goin' to want to hear all about rictus-grinnin' dead druggies, it be my boy, Mus.

Mus?

Top of it all, that boy sleep in a <u>tent</u>, I tell no lie. He got one of them pop-up types, in the middle of his room, with a blow-up mattress and a duvet. He insane. Rest of his family leave him to it, sittin' there on the sofa, glued to their TV like he some stray dog they lettin' sleep in the side room.

From inside the tent, I see lights a-flickerin', so I know he awake. I give the side of the tent a friendly kick.

Who is it, blud?

It's me, you zombie, who d'ya think?

I hear the zip unfastenin', and out pop Mustapha's head. *Wassup?* He stand up, wrapped in his duvet, his hair all mussed up like he been asleep for a week, his big eyes blinkin' and squintin' like a mole caught in a rave. Whole place smells of sleep smell, like it full of stale dream-spittle.

I say *It's mid-afternoon, man.*

So? He shrugs and frowns, pullin' the duvet tighter round his shoulders.

You ill?

He frowns even deeper. *No.*

I'm for ever havin' this exchange with Mustaph, and, like I say, he's my best mate. He's great, when he's awake. But Mustaph reckons there ain't nothin' goin' down in the land of reality. Time is better spent wrapped up in dreams. His family's place is even barer than ours. He ain't got no Playstation nor nothin', and his three older sisters don't do nothin' to keep him psyched. No games or jokes or nothin', like he ain't part of their world. That boy always dodgin' school 'cos even when he is there he jus' dozes through the lessons.

First time I met Mustaph, he was asleep. Under a tree no less, in the park. This was back in Year 5, before I got my mutt and a sense of somethin' to do, so I'm just wanderin', lookin' out for whatever goin' down. I see a gang of Year 6 boys all laughin' and jokin', standin' roun' somethin' on the ground like it the most entertainin' thing since Wii. They gigglin' like a bunch of jokers. I see a shape curled up on the grass, gently risin' and fallin' like a dozin' beast. Then one of them boys spits on the thing on the ground. Everyone laughs. Hilarious, yeah? Then another boy spits, and in a few moments all five of 'em are phlegmin' away on what turns out to be poor ol' Mustaph. So what happen is Mustaph wake up, give a yawn and a stretch, don' even speak to the boys. He jus' wipes the spit off his face with some leaves, stands up, turns round, and climbs up the tree, like a Squirrel-Man, yeah?

We're all taken by surprise, on account of Mustaph's rapid climb. In seconds he clamberin' roun' on the upper branches. Up he goes, and up. Must be hundred feet at least. When he's found a nice little nook he make himself a nest bed among the leaves and curl back up and go back to sleep.

I'm impressed.

But, see, them Year 6 boys ain't so impressed as me. Some people round here, when they see anyone doin' somethin' a bit different to sittin' pickin' their noses or squirtin' each other with shaken cola cans, it get them all beefed up. So one of these boys calls over one of the others and he gets a leg up and he start tryin' to climb the tree himself – wantin' to get up there and spit on ol' Mustaph some more.

I'm irritated by this. I walk over and I push the boy off the tree and he fall on the ground and scrape his face in the dirt. I feel good. The biggest boy, he swaggers over, all fists and lip, and next thing I know I sock him in the face, punch him to the ground. I give him a kick in the ribs, my blood floodin' round my head. Kick him again. When somethin' make my blood boil there ain't no stoppin' me. I'm a machine switched on, goin' to do what I'm designed to do until

I'm done. I kick him again. Then one of the other boys is up in my face. I put my hands round his neck and start to throttle him. The others run away. I kick this boy's legs from under him and throw him to the ground, next to the other fool.

They stagger to their feet and run away. One of 'em stops – when he reckons he a safe enough distance – and yells *Your mum's a sponger!*

He legs it. <u>She ain't.</u> <u>She ain't no sponger.</u> I'm steamin'. I'm kickin' and punchin' the tree, my blood boilin' so the inside of my head screechin' like a old kettle. I'm growlin' and cursin' and beatin' up the tree, makin' my knuckles bleed. Why do peoples do that? Why do peoples think they can jus' come, pick a fight, insult your ma?

Teachers say I got bad blood. I overheard 'em one day, in the corridor when they was in a class with the door not properly shut. They said when Marshall O'Connor leaves school he will go to prison. They didn't say they <u>thought</u> I will go to prison. They said I <u>will</u> go to prison, like it a certainty, a certainty like good kids go to university and become rich. See? I got bad blood and that what will become of me.

Eventually, I stop beatin' up the tree and I look up and Mustaph lyin' there on his branch givin' me a slow handclap applause, like he don't have a care in the world. He gimme that lopsided grin of his, do a enormous sleepy-cat yawn, go straight back to sleep. Didn't matter how loudly I yelled, he wasn't doin' no more wakin' up. Made me smile.

Another time, same teacher said I'm sure to go to jail, I hear him tellin' another teacher that Mustaph is a <u>retard</u>. That ain't right. It is a fact that <u>retard</u> is a hate word that teachers are not allowed to use. I hear other teachers say that Mus have <u>special needs</u>, but that ain't right either. Ain't nothin' special about Mustapha's needs. His needs are simple and straight.

After that day, next time I see Mustaph strollin' down the street I introduce myself. We been besties ever since.

He loyal, for sure. I never have no need to bunch my fists when Mustaph is aroun', 'cos he don' do nothin' to wind me up. He always seem to know 'zackly what I'm thinkin' or feelin' and, man, when we have a laugh, we laugh till we break all our ribs, get me?

He shuffles to the kitchen and puts the kettle on. *So whassup, man? How comes you ain't in school?*

I could ask him the same thing, but what's the point? I tell him what went down between me and fool Ashley, gettin' hit with a suspension and all. Me and Mustaph we don' have no secrets. All sudden, I tell him about the bug crawlin' outta my ear and how I'm mad with it.

He shrugs again. He rolls the duvet up, barin' the inside of his forearm. *We all got it, man, why be stressin' so?*

Like Sis say, if the upstairs people got it bad, the downstairs people got it bad also. And the people downstairs of them too. We all got it. There are three or four red raw bumps on Mus's skin, where them little devils been picnickin' offa him. It make me feel a bit less sore.

Told you. Sis and Mustaph both have a real easy way of makin' the rough stuff feel nice and smooth.

Mustaph squeezin' a teabag into his mug. Once he gone got 'nuff tea from it he dunk it in the mug for me, weak as kitten wee. Thing with Mustaph, he don' even know it that he bein' the selfish one, 'cos his mind jus' don' think that way. He jus' savin' teabags, is all. He still got that dirty ol' duvet wrapped aroun' him, despite the heat. I wonder if he actually awake or jus' sleepwalkin'.

I been waitin' for the right moment to tell him about seein' the dead body. Seem like that moment ain't gonna come, so I jus' blurt it. *Hey, man, guess what I jus' seen? Go on. Have a guess. You'll never guess.*

He shrug. *I dunno. A tiger and a rat, playin' cards. I'm serious, boy! A dead body.*

He sip from his tea, like I jus' said it a bit overcast today.

On the floor above Sis. A druggie. Gone and overdosed.

He nod, sagely, and sip more tea.

Yo, boy I say, *they took him away on a stretcher,*

blanket over his head and all.

He blink.

Throw my arms up in despair. Is there even any point in tellin' him about Soft Stuart's face? How it looked like he bein' shanked by a murderous mob, not fallen into endless sleepiness from extra-strength smack? Thing with Mustaph is, he believe anything you tell him. He got no concept of lies. You tell him pink elephants servin' behind the counter in the corner shop, he gonna say *Oh yeah* like he seen 'em already. Only thing is, he ain't gonna have no comment to make on it. Jus' blink, look wise. Boy a fool.

Awww. I give up. *I'm gettin' outta here.* But where am I goin' to go? Back to mine and sit and wait for Mum to come home, so I can tell her I got myself another suspension?

Always overreact she gonna say. *Think with your fists. Like your—*

Like my dad.

When Marshall O'Connor leaves school, he will go to prison say those idiot teachers.

I stride over to Mustaph's door and pick up his satchel. It's packed full of spray cans.

Mus, let's go and do somethin'. Let's go do some decoratin'.

Mustaph the mos' talented graffiti artist I ever seen. It's the only thing keep that boy awake. All of the best walls in our postcode are his work.

He famous for it.

He sighs and shrugs. *I'll get dressed.*

While I'm waitin' for him, I catch one of them bugs crawlin' roun' my hips. I dunno whether it's one of Mustaph's or one of mine. I squish it. Pop like bubble-wrap. <u>Sploosh</u>. Sniff my finger. It stinks. Same stink as Soft Stuart's flat when the meat men carried him out feet first.

Five minutes later, we're outta there.

Can You Tell What It Is Yet?

We walk down, seven floors. Even when not workin',
the lift is foul. By the lift door on the ground floor
it smell like the last person to use it dropped their
kebab, vomitted, and did both kinds of toilet, before
the door jammed shut behind them.

Strike that. <u>Before the door jammed shut with
them STILL inside.</u>

Bins ain't much better. We got rubbish chutes
blocked for as long as I can remember, and the metal
communal bins never get emptied on time. If I let
Sabre loose round here, in ten minutes he come back
with a rat in his jaws.

We stroll through the small playground next to
The Finger. The swings have all been torn off their
frames, and the slide been uprooted and pushed over
so it lyin' on its side. Someone taken an axe to the
roundabout. Whole place look like some fool's mouth
after they had their teeth smashed in.

Not all the neighbourhood be a bombsite. We stroll
five minutes further till we get to the playground on
the other side of the infant school, near the big park.

We go pass through it, fillin' up with littl'uns from the school, swarmin' over all the rope swings and slides, makin' the most of the neverendin' summer. Hearin' their laughin' and screechin' bring back good vibes straight away. I can see even Mustapha losin' himself in a dopey grin. The toddlers are clamberin' over the rope frame like mini Spider-Men. The mums and dads are all chillin' on the benches, chattin' and swappin' gossip.

Even though there are a zillion kids aroun' I don' have Sabre on no lead, on account of him bein' so well-trained. He always come when called, and if I'm clickin' him to <u>heel</u> he sticks close as a stalker. When I have to, I hook him onto the extendable leash, so he can run wild and free. Only problem is, he so excitable he ties people up, runnin' all aroun' them. Once he went chasin' a squirrel and ended up tyin' himself in knots roun' a bunch of trees. He fed me that dumb googie-eyed look dogs get when they remember how titchy their brains are. Stick out his tongue and pant.

We stroll past a poster tacked to a tree, one of them LOST DOG appeals. <u>Jimbob. Family pit bull. Pure bred. Will come if you call his name or offer crisps. Generous reward.</u>

Dogs and cats been goin' missin' a lot these days. Sis reckon thieves are temptin' them into the backs of vans, sellin' them for big profit. People will steal anythin' round these parts, even your dog.

Anybody try and take Sabes goin' to have me to mess with.

School chuckin' out time is safest time for a spot of graffitiin' 'cos this is when you is most invisible. Think about it. Imagine you are a officer of the law, yeah? It midnight, streets is empty, and you see two youth with hoods up, skulkin' along with backpacks. Up to no good business, for sure. Least you goin' to do is a Stop and Search. Three thirty, four in the afternoon, streets is teemin' with kids, ain't no one gonna take no notice, long as there's no gang fights breakin' out. Safe, yeah?

So we's headin' for a big communal wall far side of the playin' fields. Anybody gon' see us sprayin' there, they jus' think we got official permission. High visibility less arrestibility, right?

First up, we pass by our friendly neighbourhood Community Police. They always stop and say hello, like they part of your innermost crew. One big fat man we call Compo (<u>Com</u>munity <u>Po</u>lice, get me?) on account of him havin' a stinkin' attitude and all. Don't get me wrong, some of them are all right, jus' wanna make sure the littl'uns are safe on the street and ain't no old ladies gettin' their bags snatched, but Compo one of these wannabe Robocops, swaggerin' in body armour and jackboots. Compo always fidgetin' with his extendable baton like he gonna make himself blind. Wishin' he have can of pepper spray tucked into his utility belt, when it jus' be aluminium water bottle, on account of protectin' the community bein' such thirsty work. Lucky for us, you can't buy pepper spray on eBay – which I'm certain is where he gets his other gear from. I mean, what kind of sane person goin' to equip a fat fool like Compo with a extendable baton?

Man, Compo always wantin' to keep a close eye on the likes of me and Mus.

Poo! I'm holdin' my nose as we walk past. *Someone gone and let one off!*

Mustaph waftin' the air in front of us, like he dispersin' the stink. *Nahh, that just ol' Compo. Always smell like that, get me?*

Compo hate it when we do this. But in public ain't nothin' he can do to us, jus' fidget with his utilities like he the cock of the walk. Compo once tried to cuff Big Auntie for bein' too loud when she was cussin' some perv who'd been followin' young girls back from school. Ain't nobody goin' to cuff Big Auntie, not least in the name of safeguardin' the neighbourhood. Compo soon enough uncuffed her and was apologizin' big time to the family and friends who was mobbin' him on all sides.

We snigger past him. *Hey, Compo, found any of them stolen dogs?*

We goin' past a bench in front of the bushes and see a beast. First up, I'm thinkin' maybe it a Rottweiler, crippled by a speedin' car, limpin' along in the shade. We get closer, curiosity leadin' our feet when our brains oughta know better. It ain't no dog. Is a man, hunched up, lookin' sick as a puddle of vomit, face like a walkin' dead, jaw hangin' loose and spit droolin' down. He's on his hands and knees. He is white as snow. White and sick. We stop to look. One arm ain't bein' used to crawl, just hangin' limp, and he got a bloodstain seepin' through his shirt sleeve. He lifts his head and gives a feeble shriek. Like he's terrified, but exhausted with it.

Mustapha goes *Mr Bush?* All surprised, like he never recognized this man until the last second. His face says he still ain't too certain. *Mr Bush?*

Figure whimper, like he ain't got no words inside of him. I'm rememberin' everythin' Sis said about hard drugs and Soft Stuart and thinkin' to myself *Oh dear.* I'm squintin' down at the blood stainin' his shirt sleeve. Like he had a needle stuck in there. Tug at Mustaph's arm to keep movin', sayin' *Druggie* and lookin' disgusted.

Mustaph shake off my grip. *Naah* he says. *Mr Bush?*

But Mr Bush ain't got nothin' to say and I repeat *He's a druggie. Come on, let's go.*

My mutt is sniffin' round druggie man's feet and whinin'. I'm clickin' my fingers at him, get him move away. I don' wan' my dog puttin' his paws on no needles.

But Mustaph say *Mr Bush ain't no druggie. He lives on the floor below. He works for the church.*

*He's always comin' roun', pesterin' about jumble sales
and tombolas and sponsored walks when I'm tryin' to
get me some sleep. The dude's a Christian. Christians
don' do no drugs.*

Hmm. *Maybe he just had a epiphany, ya get me?*

Mustaph frowns and says all dry *Yo' a funny man,
Marshmallow, ain't ya?*

Mr Bush looks like he's made a long crawl from
The Finger all the way to the park in a desperate
effort to get some clean air. His breathin' all weird
like he risen up half drowned from a swamp.

I'm thinkin' what Sis would do right now. *Mebbe
we should help him home?*

Mustaph shrugs. *Havin' dragged himself all the
way over here, he ain't gonna thank us for draggin'
him back to our stinkhole. Man needs a hospital.*

Let's at least lift him up onto the bench, yeah?

Mus shrug, bend down and get a grip under Mr
Bush's armpit. I ain't so keen to stick my fingers into
his drug-sweaty pits. His arm hangin' limp like all the
blood in it turned from blood to drug. Sick. I grab his
collar instead, and together we yank him up.

On the bench we got a better view of his face.
Drugs mess you up. His eyes look like the eyes of pig
in a slaughterhouse. His mouth hangin' open, like he
forgotten how to use his jaw muscles. Droolin'.

Out the corner of my eye I clock Compo headin'
our way. He seein' we huddled over old man on a
bench, thinkin' we up to mischief. Mustaph hates

Compo more than I do. *Let's split. Let ol' Compo do his community business.*

I ain't happy. *Mebbe we can help more?*

Mallow, what you gonna do, give him the kiss of life?

Gross. Community Police best equipped to deal with this. See us hangin' around, they goin' to try and pin a *ABC* on us – Assault 'n' Battery Charge, yeah? Like we get our kicks from bashin' up the elderly and sick.

So we split, nice and calm, leavin' Mr Bush and Compo to discuss religion together down the local A&E. I ain't gettin' involved. I'm rememberin' Soft Stuart with his toes stickin' outta the blanket, tryin' to twitch themselves back to life. Today startin' to freak me.

I say *So if Mr B ain't no druggie, what do you reckon made those marks on his arm?*

Dunno. Maybe a vampire been snackin' on him? Come on, let's do some decoratin'.

Boy can't hold no topic of conversation for more than five seconds.

Behind us, I see Compo doin' his Good Samaritan bit with Mr Bush. He got him on his feet, half carryin' him, half draggin' him back in the direction of The Finger.

Look at that. Idiot Compo takin' poor fool straight back to where he crawled from.

As we walk away, I hear Mr Bush squealin' and

tryin' to pull away. But only half of him seems to have any movement, and bullyboy Compo ain't havin' none of it. Probably figured his community responsibility is to stick the druggies back inside their drug dens, where they ain't harmin' no one but themselves. He take no notice of Mr Bush screamin' and hollerin' like he bein' led to his doom. Compo hates druggies. Compo hates everyone, but he hates druggies most of all. Removin' him from the park, and stickin' him back in The Finger is just like stickin' litter in the bin.

Mustaph don' say a word. But his eyes is followin' the scene, and his Musty brain is listenin' to his eyes. Finally he say *Come, let's find our wall.*

After a while we find it, and Mustaph sets to work. Thing is, he got this joke that only he get, jus' sprayin' his wild lines and spots of colour and shadow and mutterin' *Can you tell what it is yet? Can you tell what it is yet?* like a broken parrot. He don' give away no clues, he jus' wave his arms like a windmill and squirts, and every now and again he hands me back a can and says *emerald* or *liquid blue* or *deep turmeric* or whatever crazy colour he wants. Then all of a sudden he steps back, and <u>bam!</u> just like that <u>you know what it is</u>.

Mustapha workin' away for twenty minutes mumblin' his catchphrase. All I'm seein' is a mess of sick colours around a big white splodge like a clean white T-shirt surrounded by piles of unwashed sports

gear. Don't make no sense. Then <u>flash!</u> a vision
shoots through my mind like I'm havin' a epiphany of
my own. I know what it is.

You know, I shoulda jus' gone on back to my space
and played Xbox with little Connor O'Connor, 'cos big
bro always beats little bro. I could wind him up till he
gets mad and then I could tickle him till he gets all
giggly. We could grab some ice pops from the freezer.
Mum'd come home and I'd 'fess up to her what I
gone and done at school, and that be the worst of my
worries. She be sulky with me, and I have to try and
sweet-talk her, do chores and whatever.

Anything but this.

Mustaph steps back and holds out his arms like
he's admirin' his own genius. I step back too, 'cos
you gotta step back from a picture to get perspective,
yeah? I look up and my knees go all wobbly.

What Mustaph has painted is not a white T-shirt.
It is a white face with mad boogly eyes and a gapin'
mouth screamin'. It is Ghostface from the *Scream*
films. Surroundin' Ghostface isn't dirty soccer kit.
It's junk. Junk scattered around the bins outside
The Finger, fast-food cartons, rats. It's kids in hoods
wavin' knives. Used condoms. Bloody syringes. It's
smashed TVs, burnin' sofas. It's bugs. Bugs crawlin'
all around that junk surroundin' Ghostface.

Home sweet home.

No wonder Ghostface got a rictus scream and eyes
wide with horror, jus' like Mr Bush.

Jus' like Soft Stuart.

They both got the same look, and it ain't druggie bliss-out. They are starin' at death.

Mustaph turn around and stare at me, his eyes all glazed over like he on a trip. He seen what comin' to us, and it is one antisociable, apocalyptic breakdown.

Man, what you gone and drawn somethin' like that for?

He don't answer me. Mustaph paints what he sees.

I can see The Finger loomin' over the tops of the trees. Shadows gettin' longer and the air coolin'. I do not wanna go home.

Mr Bush got the right idea. Crawl away, as far as you can get.

Couch Potatoes

But I got the baddest feelin'. I need to be with my bro, and with Mum. They need me to be with them. Mum is goin' to give me major grief, but that don' seem so important all of a sudden. We head back.

Sabre give a whine as he slink past Mr Bush's empty bench, his fur standin' to attention on his back, and <u>he</u> give me a look that say *Oh, this ain't good, ain't good at all*. All reproachful, like I'm the one responsible for anythin' bad comin' down.

I'm askin' Mustaph a heap of questions, like *What you doin' freakin' me out drawin' horrible pictures for?*

He don't answer.

What gave you the idea that drawin' Ghostface surrounded by bugs and drugs and junk was goin' to be a fun mural for all the kids in the park?

But Muskrat ain't interested in answerin' questions at the best of times. He jus' get a glaze across his eyes like he totally inscrewable. He splits at the corner, sayin' he needin' to buy more colour for his art.

Sabreboy and me race up to our flat on the tenth

floor. The forever busted lift gives me opportunity to give my dog his exercise. Today it feel like we runnin' off the stench of Soft Stuart and Mr Bush and his gurgly epiphanies, and Mustaph's stupid paintin'.

But in my head, I'm seein' Con-Con, home alone, fingertips on his cheekbones, howlin' the long, silent scream of ... <u>what</u> exactly?

In the stairwell on our floor we pass His Majesty the Cat. His Majesty sleep almost as much as Mustaph do, and he look like he own the whole Finger. No one oughta disturb his sleep or he give you that look like you the lowest of the low and beneath contempt. One time, Sabre go up to His Maj and dare to sniff at him while he asleep. <u>Pow!</u> A paw come slappin' out, get my mutt right on his nose, so he give a yelp and leap up, all four legs off of the ground. Then His Majesty jus' curl back up and close his eyes back to sleep. Today, Sabre change his step so he walkin' on the other side of me, in case the big scary cat wake up. Man, I got a yellow dog.

Connor is slumped in front of the TV with a jam sandwich. Now I see him, safe and smudgy-faced, I readjust my own face like it just a normal Monday teatime.

Gimme a smile, bro.

He obliges with a cakehole full of jam, do his great white shark impression. Tries to bite my ankle. I pretend to bite him back, and we have a right mess.

It's cool rollin' roun' with my little bro. It my duty, but cool all the same.

After all the partyin' ended when they took Dad away, it was for ever before we had a laugh again. That was when Con-Con came along. Before Con, mostly we jus' sat roun', starin' into emptiness. But one day when I was aroun' seven Mum calls me over, strokes her belly and says *Marshy, you're going to have a little brother.* So I guessed she must have met someone else, someone other than Dad. But she never brought no one home. I guess it was casual.

Anyway, when Con-Con arrived, everything brightened up. Bringin' up babies is a messy and stinky business. Me and Mum used to roll aroun' in hysterics at some of those dirty businesses of Connor's. Man, that baby was exceedingly creative, get me? From every end. Mum taught me to change nappies, dodge puke, spoon-feed and sing lullababy all the same time. Con was one happy baby. I was happy enough, swayin' him to sleep in my arms, lookin' at his tiny face smilin' up as his eyes fell into droopiness. Three of us would lie back on the sofa, all wrapped together, fartin' and smilin' and dozin'.

Mum was runnin' roun' everywhere, shoppin', cleanin', washin' and singin', so life never stopped movin' between one week and the next. Connor got his legs and we'd run roun' makin' riots, findin' games in every corner and under every surface.

Even though Mum was tired, she never snapped at us. She was doin' part-time cleanin' to help get by, which meant me and Con got playtime with Sis. Sis had the required skill to send Connor into fits of giggles.

Sure, things wasn't the same as when Dad was there. Mum would still crawl away inside her own head. I could always tell when she was no longer with us, she was with Dad again, deep inside. I went there too. I wished that Dad was aroun' to share Con-Con with us. Dad could have had us on a shoulder each.

But you know what? He never even wrote. Not a single letter. Connor got me to teach him all the wisdoms of life. Besides Mum, I had Sis and Big Auntie watchin' out for me. These days, it's me. I'm the man of the house now.

Mum's in the kitchen starin' at the microwave as it counts down a box of Micro-Chips.

Hey, son she say. *How was school?*

School. I guess it's time to give her the good news.

I'm expectin' her to blow, but she don't say nothin'. She jus' sits, watchin' the microwave countin' down to zero. I wonder if it's like countin' up to ten, so you get chance to calm down and not respond <u>inappropriately</u>, like they teach in Management Class. I'm tryin' to figure Mum's mood. She should be wild about my gettin' the suspension, but all she says is *How long?*

I say *For the rest of the week.*

She put her hand up to her face and mumble *Again*. She don't diss me nor nothin'. She be puttin' two and two together. Maybe she think if she hadn't turned her back on me in the mornin' maybe I wouldn't have bashed up Ashley. But her addin' up would be all wrong, 'cos I'd have popped Ashley anyway. It wasn't because of her, it was the damn bug crawlin' outta my ear.

So I says *Mustapha got the bugs in his place too.* And before Mum can say another word, I add *And Sis. Sis say everybody got 'em.*

Mum sits in silence for a minute. She don't wanna talk about no bugs. Her brain is thinkin' about my future, whether or not I actually <u>got</u> one, the way I'm goin' about things. *What are you going to do about your exams, Marsh?* Her shoulders slumped, like they bearin' an invisible weight.

I exhaust her.

I change the subject. Keep changin', don' let her mind settle on the bad. *We seen Mr Bush tryin' crawl away from The Finger. Compo had to carry him back. Man was sick.*

She still don' say nothin'. I'm wonderin', should I tell her about Soft Stuart, but I don't think she gonna want to hear about no dead druggies either.

Since she started cleanin' again, she ain't been mixin' much with other folk round The Finger. I know what it is. She stressin' about settin' me a bad example.

Mum done a cleanin' job once before, but she had

to give it up, on account of the money she was makin'
bein' more than she was allowed, because of her
benefits. She'd had to do what she called <u>community
service</u>, which was a punishment for workin' so hard.
Community service was where you do work but you
don't get paid for it. Which is one of those things I
don't understand. Mum was workin' doin' the cleanin'
because she didn't have enough money. And they
made her stop workin' and do other work for no
money. Which meant she had less money and had to
spend more time away from me and Connor. I never
saw no <u>benefits</u>, jus' Con-Con wearin' my old clothes
once they was scabby and worn out.

The local paper had her picture in it, labelled her
<u>cheat</u>. But who been <u>cheated</u>?

That was when one of the kids at school called her
and I got into my first serious suspension.

<u>Your mum's a sponger.</u>

Mum. I go and give her a hug. *Don't worry about no
one from The Finger tellin' the benefits on you*. I'm
thinkin' this is what she want to hear. *We ain't got no
sneaks here. You know that.*

But she stare away from me and say *I'm worse
than you.*

I wish she would shout at me, or bash me round
the ear instead of sayin' this nastiness.

Con-Con don't hear none of this, glued to the TV.
Sabretooth is huntin' crumbs offa the floor. The late

sun shinin' in from the balcony and I imagine we in a holiday apartment somewhere with a sandy beach like Tenerife or Costa Del Somethin'. But we ain't never had no holiday for as long as I remember. Mum says we went to Jamaica when I was three. I got pictures of it in my head like an old TV programme or a dream I once had.

I plonk myself next to Con-Con on the sofa. He's watchin' some rubbish, which is good with me 'cos I've still got Mustapha's paintin' floatin' round my head, which no picture of no sandy beach managin' to shake.

I wanna play. I start ticklin' Connor's feet with my feet and punchin' his hips. He starts punchin' back and we havin' a giggle. I get hold of the remote and channel-hop, faster and faster so the images all flashin', see if we can give ourselves a fit. Con drapes himself over me and rolls his eyes and sticks his tongue out, tryin' to lick his own face, still crumby with strawberry sandwich. He makin' zombie noises like he's havin' a proper fit. I join in and we rollin' around laughin'. Sabre jumps on top of us and starts lickin' our faces and Connor does a fart, a stinker, so Sabe slinks off 'cos my dog hates farts, even though he farts really disgustin' himself.

Mum comes in with a can of air freshener, aimin' it at our bottoms, laughin'.

Why ain't you angry at me, Ma?

Connor gives a girly screech and tries to dodge

the airspray. He leaps off the sofa and ducks beneath the coffee table. I yell *Noooo!* and zigzag behind her, fleein' for the bathroom. Connor come galumphin' after me. In the bathroom we got more air freshener and I arm myself with that. We each got a pair of swimmin' goggles from playin' bath games, and we put them on. Con grabs a hold of the toilet roll and out we charge. Counter-attack. Mum don' stand a chance, especially with Sabreboy runnin' roun' and roun' her legs, trippin' her up. We get her on the floor and Con-Con wraps her up with toilet roll, like a proper Mummy. She picks up one of bro's toy soldiers and aims it at us, between her finger and thumb. She machine-guns us into retreat.

Connor rummages in the box where he store his soldiers, lookin' for a fresh weapon. Mum flops down on the sofa and I flop next to her. She drops the soldier, strokes the back of my neck with her fingers. Truce.

Ping!

Sabreboy's ears prick up and he gives a happy bark. Tea is ready.

Pitter-pat

While we diggin' into our chips in front of the TV, I
hear sirens again. I go look down from the balcony.
Another ambulance. I ain't never seen so much meat
wagon activity round our block. Those meat men
got to keep runnin' up and down our stairwell. I bet
they wishin' them people was <u>Oh Dearin</u>' on one of
them nice estates with semi-detached houses and no
broken lifts.

We listen out some more and hear the clatter-
clatter around the stairwell and shouted voices,
up, up past our floor towards the top of the block.
Sabretooth starts his whinin'. After a few minutes
the meat men come back down again. Lookin' over
the balcony, I see that this time they got another
stretcher with blanket coverin' some sad head, toes
stickin' out.

This ain't no Mr B 'cos they took the body from
a flat above ours, and he down below. All the same, I
got a sick feelin' deep inside of me, and I figure I got
no choice but to do the right thing.

Hey, bro, tell me if I miss anythin'. Back in five. I

ain't sure why, but I add *Don't go anywhere, yeah?*

Makin' my way down to Mustaph's I feel as if I'm
turnin' into my dog. Shiver run down my spine and
I need a pee. Stairwell be unusually quiet, just a
slow <u>drip drip</u> that don' seem to come from nowhere.
Like The Finger is countin' itself down, like Mum's
microwave before the big <u>ping</u>! Everythin' cooked
through.

Find myself slinkin'. <u>What, am I that freaked?</u>
Shoulders back, chest out. I ain't scared.

<u>Bang bang</u>! go my fists on the door. *Yo! Muskrat!
You in?*

A few seconds later and Mustaph's dad unbolts the
door, gives me the silent nod and goes back to the
family sofa. I go into Mustaph's room, and believe me
that boy is back inside his tent, lights out.

Mus! I yell, wake my boy up. I'm hearin' rustle
of movement, and he pop his head out the tent
like sleepin' in a tent early in the evenin' the most
natural thing in the world – 'cos to this boy it
certainly is. *Mus, I got a bad feelin', man. We gotta go
check on yo' friend Mr Bush.*

He frown. *Aww, man, I'm busy. Thinkin'.*

What's that then? Horizontal thinkin'?

The best type, yeah.

I ain't havin' none of it. I don't know which flat this
Christian geezer is at, but I'm sure as anythin' – we
got to check on him. Fast. Don' care if I disturb his

Bible-readin' or what. I just wanna see him standin'.

Mustaph yawn. *What are we now – Neighbourhood Watch?* But he headin' straight for the door, wastin' no time.

I follow him out into the corridor. My boy still in his slippers. He the only boy I know who wander round outside still wearin' slippers. But, you know, ain't no fool goin' to disrespect him. Ain't nobody mess with Mustaph these days, not because he dangerous like me, but 'cos of that boy havin' no fear. He don' know the meanin' of the word.

So we skulk down the stairwell to the floor below Mustaph's. <u>Drip drip</u> go the pipin', and he stop outside what must be Mr Bush's door. I am right – no police, no medics, nothin'. Dead silent.

I'm relieved. 'Cept it <u>dead</u> silent.

Mustaph stand starin' straight at it, like he can see through. *Well?* Muskrat shrug, like I'm expectin' just a little too much. I sigh and knock on the door.

Sound like somebody shufflin' towards us to answer, but after a few moments the door don' do no openin', so I knock again.

Silence.

Mr Bush?

Silence. I look at Muskrat and he say *Look through the letter box.*

I say *<u>You</u> look through the letter box.*

He shake his head. <u>Now</u> he wide awake. *Uh-uh.*

Like I always got to do absolutely everythin' roun'

these parts. I bend down and I lift the flap of the letter box and put my mouth to it. *Mr Bush?*

What you see? ask Mus.

I see myself gettin' in a strop with my irritatin' friend. But I put my eye to the slot, and take a good peek.

Through the hallway, I can see straight through into Mr Bush's livin' room. It still light outside, so I see his sofa nice and clear, couple of bright red cushions on it, Bible balanced on the armrest, edge of a table, bottom corner of a picture frame on the wall. Besides that, nothin'.

What you see? ask Mus.

I tilt my face up so I can see Mustaph's ugly mug. *Nothin'. He ain't home.*

You sure?

I sigh, and take another look, though it be the biggest waste of time this side of school uniform. But this second look, somethin' wrong. Only I ain't sure what. The scene look exactly the same, still no sign of Mr Bush. So, what wrong? I can't tell: picture frame, table, Bible, cushion.

Holy Mother. I got it. That <u>cushion</u> – <u>one</u> cushion.

I stare up at Mustapha. *Somebody in there, someone gone move a cushion.*

I take another look. *Ohh.* Now the second red cushion gone and be moved. *This is weird.*

Lemme see.

I step aside so he can see for himself.

Well? I say.

He look back up at me like I am some sort of simpleton. *Ain't nothin' to see.*

Ain't nobody in there movin' things around? What about the cushions?

But Mustaph jus' repeat *Ain't nothin' to see.*

I shove the fool aside and take another look. I almost fall backwards in shock. There ain't no view but blackness itself, like somebody jus' draped a curtain right across the inside of the letter box. It feels like somebody standin' there, on the other side of the wooden door, listenin'.

I wait. Put my head against the door, listen back. Mustaph listen too. *You hear that?* he whisper.

What?

Listen.

I hear it. <u>Pitter-pat.</u> <u>Pitter-pat.</u> <u>Pitter-pat.</u> On the other side of the door. Against the door.

Mustaph push me aside, put his eye to the letter box. *Ohhh* he say, *now I can see.*

What? I push Mustaph aside. The view is back – picture frame, table, Bible ... and now one of them bright red cushions lyin' on the floor.

I hammer on the door, hard as I can. *Mr Bush! Mr Bush! Open up! Mr Bush! Mr Bush!*

A door clunk open across the way and a woman pop her head out, scowlin'. I bash harder still. *He ain't well. You boys leave him in peace. Tormentin' him. Get on back to your own floor, stop disturbin'* the peace. *Some of us tryin' to watch the TV! Go on, scat! Scat!*

I ain't done. Man ain't been carried out yet by no meat men. But I remember his eyes in the park. Put my eyes to the letter box one final time.

Mr Bush?

Cushion come flyin' straight up at the inside of the letter box. *Aargh!* I fall on my ass.

It ain't no cushion.

Go on, get out of here, or I'll call the police!

I don' need tellin' twice. I'm clawin' at Mustaph's leg, tryin' to get back to my feet. *We're goin'! We're goin'!* Mus tug me up. I push him over in my hurry. We scramble.

Run! I say to Mus. *Run!*

Scat! Thieves! Scat!

We don't look back.

Pow! Pow!

What happens is, we run smack-bang into guess who?

Least, I run into him, on account of havin' the scaredest legs. I dunno what I saw in Mr Bush's flat, but it mos' def' was not a pet Chiwowow leapin' up to amputate postman fingers. Nor no bad-attitude kitty cat after slicin' off your fingertips. If Mr Bush got a pet, it ain't somethin' you buy from no petshop.

What leap up at the letter box wanted to do more than snip my fingernails. I been in battles, I ain't scared of no boy, nor no man. But what was that?

Aaargh! My heart freeze with fright when I turn the corner and leap straight up into Compo's flash-buttoned jacket.

Mustaph – who shoulda been right behind me – suddenly ain't there. I don' hear him turnin' round and fleein', don' see him sneakin' through into a neighbourly flat, or edgin' all innocent roun' the side of Compo's fat, stairwell-blockin' hips. Boy jus' gone. He a genius at makin' himself disappear.

Compo squeezin' my shoulders with his pudgy

fingers, grippin' like a vice. Fat man stronger than he look.

Well he say.

Well? I smartback.

He squeeze a little harder, glarin' at me. I glare back. He squeeze harder yet and I gasp. He smile, release his grip.

I could headbutt him and he'd drop like a sack of fat. Then one kick in the gut, I stroll away easy, he wouldn't be back on his feet for five minutes.

Mum would love that, when the proper cops turn up half an hour later, haul me off down the station.

I rub my shoulders. He likes that, steps forward, backs me into the corner. *Well* he say again, 'ticulate as well as pretty.

Place for drawin' water in the desert I say.

He sighs. *Once, I thought you and I might be friends.*

I ain't that kind of boy.

No. What kind are you? The kind that takes a keen interest in their neighbours, I hear?

If Compo half the Great Detective he reckon, The Finger would be clean of undesirables. Sadly, he like a littl'un playin' Piggy in the Middle, always turnin' in time to face the direction the ball just flew <u>from</u>.

He look down at my jeans. *All right. What have you got?*

I get it. Fool think I been dealin'.

Naughty. I wink at him. *Gonna frisk me and find out?*

Sure he says, *so you can say I touched you up. Have all the infants yelling* <u>Jimmy Savile</u> *every time I show my face. Empty them.*

I pull out my phone, hold it up, away from him. No way he's gettin' his stubbies on that.

Outta the other pocket I pull a fistful of change. Open my hand, show him. <u>Damn.</u> I slipped one of Connor's toy soldiers in there when we was messin' with Mum.

Compo snatch it, his eyes lightin' up all sarcastic, pinch it between finger and thumb, aimin' the soldier's rifle at my face. *Pow!* he mock me. *Pow! Pow!*

While he busy makin' me the fool, my thumb hardworkin' also. I bring my phone down, show him the picture of his fool face. While his piggy brain takin' that in, I press a couple more buttons. <u>Send.</u>

Sis got that now I say. *You snoop on us. We snoop on you.*

He darkens. *I know you've been dealing. Where's the gear? Is your simple friend carrying it? Is he your mule?*

Mustaph isn't simple. I'm tirin' of this. *He just ain't complicated. Why you thinkin' we dealin' anyways?*

He steps forward. No choice but to edge further back.

I saw you. In the park. One minute you're handing stuff to Mr Bush, the next minute the poor man's on another planet.

Oh, they teach you nothin' in policin' class? Only planet that man on be Planet Pain. He needed a hospital, Comp. What'd you do? Drag him back here, make it all the worse for him.

What do you mean?

You wanna knock on that man's door. Better, knock it down. Go on, call some proper police, ambulance too. I tell you, that man in trouble.

Doubt and hesitation cloudin' his ugly mug. I help him along. *Go on, Comp. You wanna help the community, man in desperate need of help right now. Number 66.*

He steps back. But before he trots off, he turns around. *Don't think I'm finished with you, O'Connor* he says. *I'll be having a word with your mother.*

Give me strength. I notice he slipped the toy soldier into his Batman belt. Add to his toy collection. I call after him. *Hey, what make you think you responsible for cleanin' up The Finger anyways?*

His chest rise and fall, like he sighin'. I notice a sadness in his eyes.

Duty he says.

And he gone.

Proboscis

Nex' thing I know I'm slammin' the door shut, inside
our own flat – safe – breathin' deep, suckin' in home
smell.

Con is curled up in Mum's lap, restin' after Play
War, nappin'. He clutchin' a Transformer like it a
teddy, and his head is rested on her belly. Ain't he too
big for that these days?

Mum catch my eye. She tries a smile, but I can tell
by the way her eyes gleamin' that she been havin' a
cry. She been thinkin' about my suspension. I open
my mouth to tell her – what? Before I even form a
word that gonna make any sense, she say *In for the
night?* Too bright. Too light. She terrified of what I
get up to when I'm outta her sight. But she scared of
sayin' so. *We can have ice cream.*

Ice cream. The only weapon she got.

She don' mention no meat wagons, no stiffs bein'
carried out on stretchers. Maybe she hopin' we ain't
noticed, don' wanna be stressin' us. Protec' us from
drugs business oozin' roun' The Finger. She always
used to say if me or Con-Con ever dip into that stuff

she goin' to put us in a kids' home, but kill us half dead first.

She think it drugs right now. She runnin' scared. Don' think straight. Think we can just ask them council bureau-cats to sort everythin'. So long as we say <u>Please</u> and <u>Thanks</u> and <u>Yes sir three bags full sir</u> everythin' gonna be sweet.

She start on about the bugs predicament. She say *Hey, Marshy, guess what? We're going to sort out this bug problem once and for all. I rang Big Auntie, and tomorrow me and her are going to see the council in person. We're going to demand they inspect the whole block, and get the lift fixed up properly this time. What do you think?*

Con-Con awake now, and Mum look from one of us to the other. I ain't givin' no approval. Con won't look up from his Transformer toy. I can see he's got a bug bite on his arm. He been scratchin'.

Now. She claps her hands together. *Who's for ice cream?* She puts her hand in her pocket and pushes a fiver in my direction. *Marshmallow? You and Sabre can do the honours.*

So tragic. Back in the day, me and the mutt wouldn't need tellin' twice. That dog actually <u>know</u> the word <u>ice cream</u> and immediately start runnin' round in circles, yappin' like a loon. There ain't nothin' Sabreboy likes more than an ice cream cone, 'cept a double ice cream cone with a flake. These days, I ain't so easily diverted. My brain grown a little bit bigger than a dog's. But I gotta think. So I play along.

All right! I break into a big, fake smile.

'Cept it ain't entirely fake, 'cos a big tub of ice cream right now is appealin' comfort. I'll think <u>better</u> with ice cream. Day been another scorcher. Time to cool things down.

Me and Sabes gallop down the stairs headin' straight for the local shops. Fresh air. Forget about Compo and bugs and drugs. Make ice cream be Top Priority Number One. Sabe trots on the spot when I tie him up outside. Corner shop sits in the shadow of The Finger, but it out of spittin' distance. I hear Sabe whinin' and frettin' as I pay the girl, 'cos he know what he got comin'. I almost whinin' myself. By the time I come out the shop, my dog is slobberatin' all over the pavement.

I walk slow as I can back to The Finger, my dog runnin' greedy circles roun' me, tryin' to hurry me on. Con-Con waves down at us from the balcony and I hold up the tub like First Prize I won in a race. Choc chip. We will have us a eatin' race.

The sun is shiftin' round to behind the block. As I'm squintin' up somethin' ain't right. A shadow is movin' around on the concrete walls. I stop in my tracks. Can't be no shadow. There ain't nothin' to cast no shadow. It's about the size and shape of a dinner plate, and movin' around and around. But it ain't no dinner plate, on account of that bein' impossible.

Make no sense. I'm standin' blinkin' up at it, ice cream tub condensatin' in my hands, like my forehead condensatin' sweat into my eyes. Cold sweat. See that shadow joined by a second shadow, movin' round the same way. I see a couple more. Nex' thing, I'm seein' five, no, <u>six</u> of 'em, dark red splodges. I cup my hands round my eyes and try to focus better.

Call me simpleton if it give you satisfaction, but at this moment I am in confusion, 'cos what I'm seein' is Mr Bush's <u>cushions</u>, movin' about on their own account, up and down the side of the tower block.

I been sniffin' too much fume from Mustaph's spray cans. I gotta be 'lucinatin'.

Cushions. Cushions from Mr B's livin' room. Cushions with legs?

You know what? <u>Ding dong!</u> <u>Call the men in white coats.</u> These be <u>bugs</u> I am lookin' at. Bugs the size of rugby balls. Freeze frame. Rewind. Zoom. I am lookin' at bugs. Like when you see 'em crawlin' aroun' the wallpaper in your bedroom. But these bugs ain't right. Like I say, they – what? Foot long? Ten inches wide? Even down here I see their nasty li'l legs wigglin' as they make their way along the wall, their suckers – what's the word? – <u>proboscis</u> feelin' aroun' like tryin' to sniff out hot fresh blood to suck.

Hungry bugs.

I see them gettin' all frisky as suddenly they begin crawlin' in one direction, headin' towards the same balcony.

It be our own balcony, with Connor still standin' at it. The bugs start headin' fast, zonin' in like they got themselves fresh scent. Connor wavin' down at me, lickin' his lips like he already slurpin' this ice cream by ozzymosis. I'm focusin' in and all of them proboscises a-twitchin' in Con-Con's direction like they slurpin' <u>him</u> by ozzymosis.

Con! I yell up into the wind.

He don't hear.

CON! I wave my arms, still holdin' the ice cream tub.

He rub his belly and lick his lips, do a little dance, wagglin' his bottom.

Bugs zonin' in on him.

Sabretooth beginnin' to realize something seriously messed up, and he whinin' next to me, trottin' from paw to paw. I start whinin' too.

CONNNN!

I pull out my phone and call Mum. Connor too young to have one of his own.

It rings and rings. <u>Pick up. Pick up.</u>

Marshy says Mum, *did you forget—*

Grab Connor! Pull him in!

Bugs suddenly stop dead.

What? says Mum.

Flat three floors below, three balconies along. Door slightly open. I see a flurry of movement. Bugs - as one - jerk in that direction. Movement is curtains drawin'. A figure in a dressin' gown. A lady.

It's Mr B's neighbour, one who yelled at me and

Mus. She all ready for bed. It when you asleep you don't know them bugs eatin' at you. Don't see 'em. Don't scratch at 'em. Asleep you is the easy prey.

Bugs suddenly sprint in that direction, a flurry of skinny bootlace legs. In seconds, they in on that balcony three floors below. On it. Dartin' one after the other through the open door, through the gap in the curtain. Into the dark.

Hello? says Mum.

I drop the ice cream.

I run. Sabretooth look at me and look at the dropped ice cream like I am a maniac. I have to call him three times before he runs to catch up with me. Good boy. It take maximum doggie willpower to desert a whole tub of gently meltin' choc chip.

I run up the stairwell two and three stairs at a time. I'm puffin' and pantin', almost ready to drop by the time I reach ours.

Mum! Mum! I dash into the kitchen and grab hold of a spatula like a fool – what am I gonna do, flip 'em to death? Chuck the spatula down, pick up the fryin' pan. <u>Better.</u> Grab the bread knife. *Mum! Grab a weapon! Quick! Quick!*

What's going on? She look like somebody jus' told her the aliens have landed, which not far wrong. I point my finger at Connor. *Bro, you stay here. Keep Sabre close. Watch the spaces beneath the door!*

Mum has grabbed hold of the heavy-duty Megalite

torch that she keep by her bed in case we ever
have burglars.

Racin' down the stairwell. Mum clamberin' behin'
me, sayin' *What's up? What is it? Is someone being
attacked?*

It's the bugs, Mum I say. *Great big killer bugs.*

What?!

Hammerin' at the door with the fryin' pan. *Open
up! Open up!* I turn roun' to my mum. *We gonna have
to break down the door. Quick, smash it with your
torch.*

Mum ain't lookin' too certain about that idea. Ain't
lookin' too certain about any of this. I'm kickin' at
the door like a ragin' donkey. It open wide. Woman
standin' there, wrapped in a dressin' gown, blinkin'
and frownin'. I dash past. My eyes dart roun' the
walls and floor. I hotfoot through to her kitchen.
Clear. Swerve to the livin' room, look behind the
furniture, under the furniture, roun' the backs of
picture frames. Mum trailin' behin' me. *Marshall,
what on earth are you doing?* She all apologetic
to the woman in the dressin' gown, who ain't
said nothin'.

Bedroom. Curtains drawn so I switch on the light.
I expec' to see giant bugs scatterin' for cover. But
there ain't nothin'. I lean under the bed. Smash
wildly with the fryin' pan on account of not wantin'
to get my arm bitten off.

Marshall! Mum yellin' at me, tuggin' my arm. Says

to the sleepy lady *I'm sorry, I'm sorry, I just don't know what's come over him.* I stand back up, drop the fry pan, grab Sleepy Lady's arms, push up the sleeves of her gown, inspectin' her arms for giant bug bites. She don't like this much, wakes up a bit, yells.

Mum grabs hold of my wrist where I got the bread knife still in my hand. She lookin' at me like I a maniac. *Drop the knife, Marshall* she says.

I drop the knife. Sleepy Lady pick it up. She wave it at me, like it <u>me</u> that the threat to her further livin' on earth. Mum holds up the torch between Sleepy Lady and me, but her eyes is fixed on my eyes even though she speakin' to the lady. *It's all right* she says. *He's not threatening you, I promise. I'm sorry, I'm really, really sorry.*

Sleepy Lady tighten her grip on the knife. *You're one of the boys harassing Mr Bush earlier! I'm calling the police!*

I need to be doin' some explainin'.

It's the bugs I say. *I saw them outside. The bugs are goin' to kill you when you asleep. Goin' to suck all your blood.*

Lady fixes me with an angry look. *You horror! Police! Police!*

No! Mum cries. She turn to me. *What is the matter with you? You're going to end up just like your fa—* She checks herself.

I look down from her dagger eyes. I get it. Mum think I'm outta control. She think my anger issues gone off like a scatter-bomb. *I seen 'em, Mum* I say desperately.

She grabs me by the elbow. *I'm really sorry* she says to Sleepy Lady again. I give up. They ain't goin' to believe anythin' I say.

Mum start leadin' me out. *I'm sorry* she says again. She jus' can't get enough apologizin' outta her mouth. It's humiliatin' for the both of us.

Jus' before she yank me outta the flat, I see Sleepy Lady got three or four bullet holes along the wall, like gangsters been here, shootin' the place up. <u>Blam.</u> <u>Blam.</u> <u>Blam.</u> Don' make no sense.

Mum draggin' me along the hallway, hurtin' my arm. When we get to the corner, we see Sis watchin' us from the doorway. I pull myself outta Mum's grip. *Sis!* I say. *I gotta talk with you.*

Mum lets me go, but she look terrified. *Will you watch him for a minute?* She's lookin' back at Sleepy Lady, who already tappin' numbers into her phone. *You see if you can't talk sense into my boy!*

Sis give Mum her sympathetic smile. Mum seems to surrender, and turns back to Sleepy Lady. *Let's calm down* she says to her. *Let's talk this through for a minute.*

Come Sis say to me, guidin' me up towards her floor.

Mum turn round one last time. *I want you in your bed within the hour, boy. You hear? In bed. Asleep.*

You know what? I have the very best intention

of stayin' up late as I possible can. I ain't shuttin'
my eyes ever again. Not with these blood-suckin'
monsters crawlin' roun' the block.

Shut your eyes, boy, you gonna die. We all gonna
die. Jus' nobody else know it yet.

The Terrible Facts

Mum figure I'm safe stayin' with Sis until I get
myself calm down. Sis only a year older than me, but
Mum ain't stressin' at me spendin' time alone at her
place. Sis ain't that kind of girl.

Sis the only one of my crew with a smartphone.
I got a dumbphone, has a camera, that about it.
Mustaph so down, his family got one of them meters
for the TV, where you put in the pound coin for 60
minutes of Britain Got Talent.

Sis one of them families in The Finger that never
have any money but always has everythin' they need.
Big Auntie clever like that. I need Internet to find
out 'zackly what we up against. Sis got it all on her
BlackBerry.

First off, Sis demandin' to know what's been
kickin' off. I spill all in a mad rush. She be laughin'
first up. But I can tell it nervous laughter. Sis know
me long and deep enough that I ain't drug-crazed or
bent in the head. But she saw everything kickin' off
outside Sleepy Lady's flat.

Marsh, you ain't been on the same gear as

Soft Stuart been?

I throw her disgust. I know she jokin', but she know me better than to even try that sort of wit. Bad enough Mum stressin' about such nonsense.

Listen, boy, I ain't doubtin' what you think you saw, I swear I ain't, but you talkin' a tale of giant bloodsuckin' monsters, yeah? You ain't gettin' nowhere without no proof.

Do you need proof, Sis?

Listen, Marshy. This girl needs proof of everythin'. You ain't survivin' nothin' in this life if you jus' accept everythin' that thrown at you. Some days I need proof I'm even here. I believe you believe what you seen, but until I see anythin' with eyes of my own, I ain't believin' nothin', get me?

Sis always been the smartest person I know. Teachers hated her at school 'cos she used to sit and say *Show me the proof.* Teachers would draw her the pictures, she say *Just a picture, man. How do I know you ain't just made it up? Come on, show me the proof. Show me the proof.*

Imagine bein' a teacher havin' to stand that all day long. They called her out for bein' a wind-up, but thing with Sis is, she's a hundred per cent genuine. I'm good with that.

I say *You seen the bodies gettin' carried out, yeah?*

Sure. Soft Stuart. Man was a walkin' pharmacy. Now he a lyin'-down pharmacy.

What about the other one, taken out early this

evenin'. Him too? And what about Mr Bush?

What about him?

Me and Mustaph seen the bugs movin' around in his flat. And I seen 'em crawlin' round on the outside walls.

Didn't realize until this minute how desperate I am to be believed.

Sis smile, ain't risin' to it. *I gotta see proof of my own, is all. Listen, bro, if it helps, I reckoned I saw somethin' scurryin' around Soft Stuart's. I was thinkin' it must be a nasty ol' rat. But, you know, rats ... bugs...*

Yes! Thank you.

Well, Sis, what we goin' to do?

She folds her arms. *Your mum already classin' you Fool of The Finger. What do you think Big Auntie goin' to think?*

I already tried to catch one of them bugs, all it did was make Mum sore at me.

Sis give me her sweet smile. *You gonna have to try a bit harder, ain't you?*

I need your assistance, Sis. I need to think like the Big Game Hunter, get me? Need to understand my foe.

That my boy. What's your plan?

I shrug. She already on her phone, searchin' for <u>bedbugs</u> so we can arm ourselves with info.

Believe, this info is ten out of ten on the Scare-o-meter.

First up Sis reads out, *both male and female*

bedbugs feed on human blood. Right. They use our blood to shed their baby shells and grow nice new shiny ones.

I'm peerin' down at the phone. Can't believe how many websites there are for bedbugs.

We know that true I say. *We got the bite marks remindin' us.*

Sis goes on. *They breed at a phenomenal rate. Lay up to twelve eggs per day. Eggs coated with sticky substance so they adhere to the surface. Eggs hatch around ten days. Nymphs immediately begin to feed.*

Hold up right there I say. *What's a nymph?*

She smile at me. *A little one. A baby. Says here they require a blood meal in order to moult and develop into the next stage.*

Right about now me and Sis lookin' at each other with widescreen eyes. Twelve eggs a day and them little baby nymphs feastin' on our flesh rightaways. I itch jus' hearin' it.

There's more. *Adults grow to ten to twelve millimetres. Bedbugs have an extremely tough exoskeleton. Most current pesticides won't penetrate this exoskeleton.*

Exoskeletons? I blink at Sis like a fool. *These guys sound like Armageddon critters.*

And guess what? They hide out durin' the day, and when night come ... well, bedbugs are attracted to body heat and the carbon dioxide in expired air, which is how they find their host. Devious, yeah?

What you tellin' me, Sis, is that they <u>sniff</u> us out.
Hunters. They know 'zackly where you be
snoozin' away, but you can't feel nothin' when they
bite, on account of them injectin' an <u>anaesthetic</u>.
Then they inject an <u>anti-coagulant</u>, which thin out
your blood, make it runny for suckin' up nozzles.
You followin'?

I wish I wasn't. I feel sick.

Sis reads more. *As the bedbug engorges, it*
changes from light brown to rust-red. Whoahh! We
get paler, they get redder, fillin' up with our juice.
They suck for <u>ten minutes</u> or so. Crazy itchin' only
happen an hour later, once the damage all done. They
crawl somewhere nice and dark to digest their slap-
up meal. Marsh, you OK? You lookin' pale.

We leanin' closer into each other. Sis is scratchin'
at her arm.

Listen, Sis, these Megabugs, they ain't ten milli-
metres long, they ten <u>inches</u> long. When they slurpin'
your good stuff, they takin' ten times as much.
Imagine five or six of them on you. You be literally
dead meat.

I'm thinkin' of Soft Stuart, empty, bloodless like a
sucked-out ice-pop wrapper. I'm hopin' Sis thinkin'
the same, but she shake her head, like her brain just
ain't havin' it. *Naah. No way, man. Marshmallow,*
these bugsies are nasty critters, ain't no arguin', and
maybe you seen some pretty mean-lookin' ones, but -
naah. No way. We jus' got a infestation, is all.

I thought you believed me, Sis.

She shake her head. *Listen, Marsh. Tomorrow your mum and my mum goin' to teach those council peoples a thing or two about infestations. You get me? Those council men be cleanin' this place from top to bottom. We ain't goin' to have no bugs suckin' away at us. Don't know what you saw, but trust me, giant bugs ain't it. Chill, boy.*

She be yawnin'. I guess this my hint to leave. I ain't takin' it.

I saw them, Sis. We're in danger. All of us. I can't protect the whole Finger on my own.

She tired of this, her voice toughenin' up like Mum when she nearin' the end of her tether. *Listen up, place as skanky as The Finger goin' to be hostin' the ugliest bugs in the city. But ain't no Megabugs I'm seein'. Who gonna believe you, yeah? If you ain't got no evidence, you ain't got jack.*

Evidence. Only one way I'm gettin' any evidence. The same way by which I ain't turnin' into no Bug Supper. By stayin' awake. By stayin' up all night, keepin' watch on my little bro and Ma, and waitin' for one of them beauties to make an appearance. I will splat that sucker all over the walls.

But I'm worried. If Sis don't believe, she ain't gonna protect herself.

Sis, you got to promise to stay awake too.

She sighs. *Marshmallow, last thing you oughta be doin' is stayin' awake. You stressed, boy. You be needin' proper rest.*

I fix her the evils. I can't believe she still ain't takin' this serious. I punch the door. <u>Thud.</u> That feel fine.

What you doin'?!

I punch it again. <u>Thud.</u> Feel real good. Graze my knuckle.

Stop it, Marsh!

You think I'm mental? I punch it again.

She grab my arm. *Stop it!*

AWAKE! I'm writhin' out of her grip. *YOU STAY AWAKE!*

She takin' me serious now. *Boy, you crazy* she say, but suddenly she on red alert.

You listenin' to me? My face in her face. *You listenin' to me?*

Yeah she nod. I don' know. I don' know if she think I'm headin' for the loony bin.

How far back we go?

We go back she admit.

My fist throbbin', knuckles sizzlin' like they got 'lectricity flowin' through. My friend ain't gonna get sucked to death by no giant bugs. My fist ain't goin' to allow it.

How far?

Her eyes take that steely look. We sharin' enough knowledge. More than words.

You got me now? I ask.

I got you.

You goin' stay awake now?

She places her hand over my fists. I feel my knuckles tinglin' into her palm. *Marsh, you know well enough that I always sleep with one eye open. But let me reassure you, I got a secret weapon all of my own.*

Make sure I believe, she leads me through to the kitchen, reaches under the sink. Pulls out a spray can. On it is DOKTOR DOOM.

Bug spray. I laugh. She lightened the mood. *Sis, that's for <u>normal</u> bugs. These guys are monsters. Bug spray ain't goin' to kill none of them.*

She winks. *Maybe not, but if I spray it round my bed, it'll put them off enough to go searchin' for easier meat elsewhere, yeah?*

She got a point. We touch knuckles. Next up, I need to warn Mustaph, but before I head out, I scribble two notes, to push through the letter boxes of Mr Christian and Sleepy Lady. Each note say the same thing:

<u>Don't sleep.</u>

Sure, I Believe You

I head down from Sis's floor, and jus' before I turn
the corner onto ours, I hear voices. I tiptoe to the
corner, and stop, and listen.

It ain't my nature to be sneakin' roun', but one of
the voices I'm hearin' is Compo's.

The other voice is my mum's.

I guess Sleepy Lady called the Law after all. Lucky
for me, Compo was the best they could muster. He
ain't exactly Dirty Harry. But I bet he fillin' Mum's
head with all kind of dirt on me.

Can't quite catch what they sayin', all hush hush.
So I poke my head roun' the corner jus' for a sec.

Comp is in our doorway, handin' something to
Mum. Look like a letter. Same size and shape as
the letter she was readin' this mornin', got a fancy
logo on the back like it from somebody official. Why
she showin' it to Compo? What's the big whisperin'
deal?

I wait until I hear our door click close, and Compo
ploddin' back down the stairwell.

Make my way down to my boy.

Sure says Mustaph, *giant bugs.*

Thank you. Somebody else believe. Now we gettin' somewhere. *You seen 'em too?*

Mustaph stare blankly back. *No.*

But you – what? You seen them attack someone?

No.

You believe me though? What we saw at Mr B's?

Mus frown, lookin' puzzled. *What, those cushions?*

No! I throw my hands up. *The cushions were bugs!*

Bugs?

<u>*Yes.*</u>

The cushions we saw … were bugs?

<u>*Yes!*</u>

Oh, OK.

Put my head in my arms and count to ten. My only option. Deep breath. *Mus* I beseech. *Do you understand what I'm sayin'?*

Sure. You're sayin' the cushions we saw at Mr B's weren't cushions at all. They were giant bugs.

He nod his head to show he got hundred per cent acceptance.

Great. The only person who believe me is someone who'd believe your fingers were fish if you told him air was water. Mustaph would accept Dizzee Rascal was King of England if you told him with a straight face. He'd accept it if you told him with your hands coverin' your mouth to hide the giggles.

<u>Mr Bush's sofa cushions are giant man-eatin'</u>
<u>bedbugs.</u>

Well, of course.

Maybe Sis is right. Maybe I am jus' too wiped. Mum can call me a liar. Sleepy Lady can threaten me with the police, and Sis can ask me to take a proper logical look at myself. None of that matter, I'm safe with my conviction. But the moment Mustapha the Wise One agreein' with me, I feel like I have it totally wrong. *Aaaaaaarrrghhh...*

Wassup? say Mus, dunkin' his teabag in and out of his mug. Same teabag as earlier. He gettin' value for money. *You worried the giant bedbugs are goin' to eat us all alive?*

Yes I whisper. Think I'm goin' to sob like a baby.

Ahh he say, suddenly gettin' it, *that's why you told us to run for our lives?*

Yes.

He twirlin' his teabag round and round on its little string while he ponders this. *So ... they the same as the little bedbugs, only bigger?*

Yes! Think I'm goin' to slit my wrists with frustration.

They goin' to suck out all our blood while we sleepin', only this time we ain't doin' no wakin' up?

Yes.

He sups his tea. *Well, in that case I ain't goin' to sleep.* Consequence of this dawns on him. *Aww, man, no sleep! That's a shame. Sleep is the sweetest thing I got.*

I say *You better brew yourself a stronger cup than that if you wanna stay awake all night.*

Oh, I will, I will. He wink at me. *You know what? I got me a secret weapon.*

For a moment I think to myself, maybe if Mustaph is my only ally, that's better than nobody, and maybe he can come up with somethin' more useful than a can of DOKTOR DOOM, yeah?

What is it?

He blow on his tea. <u>It's already cold!</u> I will throttle him.

What is your secret weapon, Mus?

It's a secret. He wink at me again.

Mus?

He look at me and sip his cold, watery tea.

Why d'you believe me about the giant bedbugs?

Put down his mug, peer into my eyes. *You on hallucinatories?*

You know I don't do that stuff.

And you my best friend, yeah?

You know it.

Ain't gonna tell me no lies then, is you.

That's it. Ain't no more to say. I'm not alone.

Don't Sleep

11 p.m. I down Red Bull. I ain't actually in need
of it. I am so wired, I'm leapin' outta my skin at
every creak.

Here's me back in my bedroom, but I ain't got no
intention of goin' to bed. Mum already in bed when
I got in. Checked on her straight away. No bugs. I
stood by her door, watched for a few minutes as my
eyes got used to the dark. Think she was awake, 'cos I
couldn't hear no sleep-breathin'. Think she was lyin'
there, fumin'. Neither of us said nothin'.

Woke up Con-Con. He think I'm goin' Lady Gaga.
Wants to know all about giant bedbugs like it a
littl'un's bedtime story. Gobble up the gory detail.

12 midnight I drain a can of Hype. Still ain't
needin' it. Buzzin' like a 'lectric fence. Bruv keep
makin' slurpin' noises from beneath his sheet then
gigglin' like a fool, like it the funniest joke ever
in history.

Check on Mum. She is restin' now.

1 a.m. I down the XS. Walkin' roun' and roun'
on the spot, wearin' a hole in the lino. Why we got

lino? Why no soft carpet? Giant bugs can come crawl through the cracks in the lino. If they hungry enough, they be flat enough. If they flat enough, they can be hidin' anywhere. Start feelin' roun' behin' all mine and Con-Con's posters. Spyin' under Con-Con's bed. Con-Con no longer seein' the funny side. He still awake, but preten' to be asleep. Tickle his feet. He kick me in the side of the head. That my boy.

2 a.m. I gulp down the Crunk. What kinda name that for a sof' drink? *Crunk.* What goes *Ha Ha Ha – Crunk?* Man laughin' his head off.

Little brother now snorin' away. Check behind posters again. Pull up the edges of the lino, shine the torch through the gap, squint down, see what I can spot. Look under Con-Con's bed. Remember I forgot to look under <u>my</u> bed. Pick up the fryin' pan and stick my head under. Search behind every bit of clutter. Gotta de-clutter. Too much clutter bad for you. Hear a rustlin' in the closet and pull the door open double-quick to surprise the monsters. It packed with junk. Rip down the mountain of toys, 'cos that where they could be hidin' themselves. <u>Clatter smash bang</u>, all come tumblin' down. Con-Con sigh and sit up in his bed. *Marsh, go to sleep! Be quiet, man, you're crazy.*

He not think I so crazy when I stop the bloodsuckers from emptyin' out his arms and legs.

3 a.m. Still no giant bugs. Too wired to need to swig the Blufrog. Will save it for later when tiredness kickin' at me. I've pulled out the old photo I have of

Dad from beneath my mattress, losin' myself, thinkin' about the old days. Picture at a funfair we visited. Three of us on a old-school carousel. Pretty painted horses swirlin' us roun' and aroun'. Me in the middle with my arms raised. Mum and Dad got theirs raised too, holdin' mine up like a Champion Prince. Dad looks like a old swashbucklin' pirate and Mum a movie queen. Happy Days.

This day, normal-sized bugs be grievin' me, attackin' on all fronts. I got itch bumps along my back and arms and legs. Decide I'm goin' to hunt for them as well as their giant cousins. Shouldn't be hard, as they usually swarmin' over my bedsheet like players on a soccer pitch. I've squished seven of them, pop 'em between my fingers like bubble wrap. Sploosh. I'm makin' a pile in one of Mum's ashtrays. It be a warnin' for their big cousins. I pull down my beddin' and there be a whole crew of them makin' a break for it along the bedsheet. I squish squish squish. Stinky and messy. I brush my fingers against each other so the body parts all fall onto my Warnin' Pile. Remember that bugs love books, love doin' their business on the page corners. I grab Con-Con's Harry Potters, shake 'em out one by one. Splat. Splat. Fingers a stinkin' mess. Didn't think this through. Tell myself *Don't sniff 'em, don't sniff 'em*, but it like when you wipe dead skin from between yo' little toes. Who in the world got the willpower to resist? The smell similar, but bug smell more bitter, pungent.

Second-hand blood.

Go to the bathroom, <u>scrub scrub</u>. Grab Mum's nail-file from the cabinet. From now on, the little bugs get the bayonet treatment.

4 a.m. Call my dog, nice and quiet, rummage his fur for creepies. Sabre look at me like *Why you doin' this in the middle of the night, boy?* Believe me, my dog truly used to be a dirt machine. I 'member before Mum called in PEST CONTROL, Sabre itchin' and scratchin' like he the Big Top for a flea circus. When I got my face right in there it wasn't fleas leapin' about. It was bugs, all bubbled up with blood like he jus' some furry ol' KFC Family Bucket for Mr and Mrs Bug and their buglets. My dog deserve better. From then, I gave my dog weekly baths.

Wasn't no use. Me and Connor clean as licked plates, dog shinin' like a Prize Winner, and PEST CONTROL intoxicated every inch of the place. <u>Still</u> them bugs came back, with a grudge and extra gang members.

Bigger and most definitely badder.

When I pick three of the little ones off of Sabe's belly fur and show him the culprits he try and eat the dead ones, but the taste too nasty even for him.

I hear a noise. I swear I hear a <u>pitter-pat</u> from Mum's room. Smack my forehead. I am a fool. Ain't checked on her for – how long? Pick up the fry pan. Tiptoe to her room. Only light, the light from my torch. I see shape of Mum beneath her duvet. No movement. I shine the torch across the floor. No sign of any Megas.

Mum?

She don' say nothin'. She either asleep or dead.

I sniff the air, searchin' for their musty stink.

Mum?

Damn, I left it too late. Sweatin' now. What am I gonna do? If Mum is dead and Dad is gone away in prison, who gonna watch for me an' Connor?

Me. I'll watch Connor.

Who gonna watch for me?

Mum?

Listen. Listen deep. I can't hear no breathin'. I can't hear no bug <u>pitter-pat</u>.

Lean close. I can't see no movin' beneath the duvet where her chest be breathin'. She ain't breathin'. Can't see her face. She got the duvet pulled up. Like Soft Stuart on the stretcher to the meat wagon, just his toes stickin' out.

Dead.

I hear rustlin'. Look down where her legs at, and the duvet has started movin', all weird. Can't breathe. Everythin' caught in my throat, like trapped meat. Squeeze my swollen knuckle roun' the handle of the fry pan. Slow, smooth, pull up the bottom of the duvet, revealin' her toes, her ankles, now her knees.

No Megabug.

She shifts her leg, bends her knee. *Marsh?* Slappin' her lips together like she half awake. She was jus' changin' position in her sleep.

Damn. She gonna kill me. I ease the duvet back over her feet. Listen close. Hear her breathe deep sleep-breath.

I hear the pitter-pat, comin' now from mine and Con-Con's room. Sabretooth givin' a whimper.

This is it. We under attack. My heart hammerin' like a house party in my chest. Legs won't move. I look down, see if they been paralyzed by demon bug bites. But it fear gone and paralyzed them. Move!

I almos' barge into Mum's dressin' table dartin' out from her room. I'm gonna club with my torch and splat with the fry pan. If I hit the Megas direct, one blow is all it'll take. Stun 'em, give me time to go for the kill. Boom boom my heart.

Get to our room, nothin' here. Sabretooth sittin' tremblin' like Scooby Dooby Doo, startled round-eyed look on his face. He wag his tail, slink towards me on his belly, like he thinkin' it's him I'm gonna clatter over the head like a baby seal.

Check the whole room again for Megas, cussin' my dog. Sabre lookin' shamefaced and cowardly. Dog that cried wolf.

I can't be two places at once. Sabe got to stay awake too and keep guard. Drag him back through to Mum's room, shut him in. If Megas goin' to invade the room, they'll suck at the dog first. He can howl the alarm before they start suckin' on Mum.

Sorry, boy. Promise I'll check on you.

5 a.m. Connor snorin' away. Quiet as a bug myself, I pull down his sheets so's not to wake him. He wearin' a T-shirt and boxers. His arms and legs are polka-dotted by bug bites. Five or six crawlin' on him. Make me quietly go nuts, 'cos Connor's blood be swellin' their bodies. <u>Every night they suck my bruv's blood, and mine, and Mum's.</u>

They also suckin' at Mustaph, and Sis, and Big Auntie. All I know, they suckin' at everyone in the whole block. No one able to stop them.

And now big bugs. Megabugs, to suck us good and dry.

Don't nod off. Don't close eyes. Do your duty.

6 a.m. Guzzle the last can, Blufrog. Check on Mum. Sun risin'. Sweet. No Megas. Shinin' torch in corners, patrollin' posters and books, pillows, mattresses – check seams, check for holes, go through clothes drawer, shake out my gear, shake out Con-Con's socks and boxers. No more bugs. No Megabugs. Don't sleep. Don't.

7 a.m. Connor saying *Marsh?*

Was I asleep? Am I bit?

Marsh?

I nodded out, but it OK. Check myself. No Megas. Check bruv.

Why you lookin' at me like that, Marsh? You losin' it, bruv.

Maybe. But it be mornin'. We survived. We all right.

Bullets For Breakfast

I take a shower, wake me up, wash off my warpath smell.
When I come out, Mum makin' Con-Con toast and I
can tell she got the hump big time. Maybe she mad
enough over Sleepy Lady, maybe for me bangin' on
about bugs, maybe for gettin' me another suspension,
but mostly 'cos big-mouth Connor tell her I sat up all
night drinkin' pop.

She keep glancin' at the space on the wall where
we had the picture of Dad, which I put up when we
moved in. She took it down not long after. In her
head the photo still there – 'cos when she's stressed I
see her lookin' at it. At the empty space.

She don' know I fished that photo out of the junk
drawer. My own eyes get to rest on it whenever
they please.

Con leaves the room, get ready for school. I'm
butterin' toast for me and my dog. Mum starin' at me,
dead-eyed. Sound of the knife spreadin' marge across
the toast scrapin' across the silence, louder than it
oughta, like a bug back inside my ear, scrunchin' at
my brains.

Mum, dead-eyed.

Like she doin' her microwave countdown from ten so her temper don' explode. Wait for the ping. There ain't no ping. She get to zero. Minus one. Minus two. Scrape scrape. Minus three. Minus four. Bug chewin' my ear. Minus five...

What? I throw down the knife.

She stare down at the knife. Look up from the knife to my face. From the blade to my eyes.

What?

Marsh... Her head still countin'. Minus six. Minus seven. *Marsh ... what were you looking for in Mrs Lalwani's flat?*

Mrs Lalwani. Guess that's Sleepy Lady.

What am I supposed to say? *I told you.*

Marshall she say, fingerin' a tea towel in her hand, fidgetin' like worry beads, *did Mr Bush owe you money?*

What?

She look away from me. *They say it sounded like you were hassling him. Was it – was it payment?*

Mum, what are you talkin' about?

She won't look at me. Can't look at me.

I see. *Is that what Compo said?*

She reaches across the table, puts her hand over mine. Now she's gazin' at me proper deep. *Officer Cotton told me he's concerned about you...*

I pull away, jump to my feet. Officer Cotton. *Compo don't know jack!*

Marshall, please...

This what I get? This my thanks? This what
happens when I do what I got to do as eldest of
the house?

*Marshall, Officer Cotton couldn't do anything for
Mr Bush. He was already dead...*

<u>Already dead.</u> The words sink in. I failed. Did too
little, too late.

It was overdose, Marshall. Bad drugs.

Oh dear oh dear oh dear what are we goin' to do?
What? What?

Mum is goin' on. *Why did you stay up all night?*
And on. *If you're on something, you can tell me –
please?* And on. *Marsh, are you involved with dealers?*

I ain't hearin' this. I'm outta the room.

In the livin' room I'm throwin' cushions.

I'm starin' at nothin'.

Mum starin' through me. She still holdin' the
tea towel, stop her hands doin' what she don' want
them to.

I'm thinkin' about Dad.

Connor comes through, dressed for school. *Hey,
Mum* he say, *you ain't goin' to believe this. We got
bullet holes all across our wall.*

Nice one, cheesebag. Bro hates me and Mum
diggin' at each other. Play the joker, lighten the vibe.

*Connor, I have serious dealings with your brother.
Last thing I need is you adding your own nonsense.*

But my bruv got a twisted look. Remind me of the

time he wet the bed, came in lookin' all fearful, eyes like egg yolk. *It's true* he say. *Come see.*

Mum toss down her tea towel and throw me a quick glance as if to say *Don't think I've finished with you, boy.* I follow her into the bedroom.

Sure enough – <u>bullet holes</u>. A wobbly line of 'em near the ceilin', like MechAssault 2 been played out for real, in our room.

Mum start tremblin', real bad. I never seen this before. She start freakin', soon as she seen the bullet holes, hand shakin' like she been sittin' in a deep freeze. *My handbag* she mutters, her voice all croaky. *Marshall, my handbag – now.* She don' look at me as she gives her order – can't take her eyes off the line of bullet holes on the wall.

I dash to the kitchen, get her bag, but somethin' ain't right. I seen these bullet holes before somewhere.

Why you need your handbag?

She fumblin' round in a panic, spillin' make-up and hairbrushes and tissues. *Emergency number* she says, almos' to herself. *I warned them something like this would happen...*

Emergency number? Bullet holes? I am in confusion. I pull up a chair and I stand on it, stretch an arm up towards the holes.

Behind me, Mum is sayin' *It's why you pulled Connor in from the balcony, isn't it? Because—*

My heart stops. *These ain't bullet holes.* I scratch at one of them. It's like black paint, same size and shape as a bullet hole. But it scrapes away under my nail. I sniff it, wrinkle my nose.

What? say Con.

Who are you mixed up with? say Mum.

I know for sure Mum ain't goin' to take this well, but I say it anyway. What choice do I have?

Ain't no bullet hole.

What? Con repeat.

It's giant bug poo.

I hold out my finger, so they can take a sniff. Giant bugs paid us a night visit after all.

Mum says she's goin' to get me to see a <u>specialist</u>.

Did you <u>paint</u> these? she say.

What, she think I am that twisted?

She say *How can I cope, bringing you up on half a wage, place as busted up as The Finger, worrying about your dad, and here you are with – what? With <u>deep psychological problems</u>.*

She turn and look at Con-Con. *Please* she plead at him, *don't follow your brother—*

I go ape. *I ain't got no deep psycho problems, I jus' got eyes in my head, brain behind my eyes. You can't admit evidence that in front of your face, you got the problem!*

Con-Con place a pile of books on top of the chair, help him reach, scratchin' away at the holes himself. *Bug poo.* Sniffin' at his fingers. *Giant bug poo.* Can't keep how impressed he is out of his voice. *How big*

*are the bugs, Marsh? Are they as big as the TV?
Bigger than Sabretooth?*

In the centre of us all goin' ape and bein' struck
awesome, I got a voice in my head, askin' me over
and over *Why's she stressin' about Dad right now?
What's she doin' with a* <u>*emergency number*</u> *in her
bag? Why's she believe them was actual bullet holes?*

I didn't mean to do no tippin' her over the edge.

I talk soft. *I'm tryin' to do right, Ma. Watch out for
us all.*

Before she can answer me, we hear the sirens.

Seems like the sirens comin' straight out of her
head, 'cos my own head is buzzin' from the energy
drinks and lack of sleep, and my mum is in a
emergency situation. Riot squads blazin' inside her.

But no. Sirens are from down below. Mum jolts
like a bolt of electricity shot through her. We all rush
to the balcony, see what's happenin'.

Meat wagons. My voice say the words all flat.
Tricky to be pleased with yourself when dead people
happenin' all over your zone.

Go back inside, Connor. Mum don't want him to
see this.

Uh-unh. He ain't goin' nowhere. We're peerin' over
the balcony, we got police, we got ambulance. I ain't
happy to be proven right.

Is it a dead person? Con's eyes fix on a stretcher
bein' carried over to a meat wagon.

It is a dead person.

Go inside Mum insists. He pretends not to hear.

It gets worse.

Two more stretchers come out, followed by grievin' grown-ups. Mr and Mrs Vertov. I know them, their kids go to Connor's school. I notice the stretchers, each one carryin' only half a load.

Get inside! I snap at Connor.

I seen these littl'uns playin' in the park when we gone taggin'. Leo and Lola, brother and sister. They don't even half fill the space on the stretcher, jus' skinny things.

Empties.

What, now? I glare at Mum. *You goin' to be sayin' that they done hard-druggin' also?*

Ambulance men bring out yet another stretcher. This one give us the nastiest surprise. As they struggle to lift the stretcher into the back of the wagon after carryin' the weight down all them stairs, one of the men slip and the stretcher tilts, almos' drops. Death blanket falls away from the corpse's face. Flat out on this stretcher is one Sleepy Lady. She havin' a lot more than 40 winks. I look at Mum and she look at me, and we both thinkin' the same thing. We thinkin' about when we was in Sleepy Lady's flat. Was we the last people to see her while blood still flowin' through her veins?

This be anywhere else in the city, all these dead bodies gettin' carried out the same building, place'd be crawlin' with Papa Ratzis, takin' gruesome pics

and all. But ain't no media raisin' an interest in a
bunch of dead scuzzies like us.

Meat wagon drive away. Sirens switched off.

I'm thinkin' of Con-Con. My watchin' over him
through the night. Him full of sauce those Megabugs
wanna slurp up, drain right out of him.

Meanwhile, we left Sleepy Lady alone, become Bug
Supper.

Mum lookin' at me like it all my fault. Like
I shoulda done more. But words comin' out her
mouth make no sense. *Marshall, what have you got
involved in?*

I blink.

What did you do to her?

Sleepy Lady? No. Not me. I did my best.

You have to hand yourself in. Tear trickle down
her cheek. *I will come with you. To the police station.*

No.

I turn, run out of the house.

The Attic Office

Think I'm gonna puke. Got the sweats. Everythin'
spinnin'. Get right away from home. How can she?
Run. Air. Need to breathe. How can she think that?

I'm runnin'. Up. Up. The only way out of here. She
think I'm plannin' a badman's life. She think I'm
runnin' with the wrong crew. My own mum. Need air.
Up, up.

I know where to go.

Day pass by, shadow of The Finger spread itself
far as you can see. Ain't no escapin' it. Only way to
be not touched by it, and that to rise above. So I run,
up, faster than my stomach can rise up to my throat,
keepin' the sickness down. Spinnin' round and round
the stairwell. Dizzy. East and west, left and right.
Higher and higher. Round and round. *Marsh, are you
- my own mum - you are, Marsh - round and round -
involved with dealers?*

Me and Con and Mus and Sis, we don' go up
the top floor of The Finger too much. The top floor
flats are empty, desolated, on account of the damp.
Windows up top drippin', like eyes been bitter

weepin'. Few times we adventured up there recent months, we seen people sexin' each other, seen people wild on illegals, one time even dog-fightin'. So we don' go up, not too often now. Top of the block is the pits, if that make enough sense for you.

But we know a space on top of all those ruined flats. Secret space. You go round a little corner, see what look like a cleaner's cupboard. Always shut, but not locked. You go through it, climb more steps, and you in the Attic Office.

Only me and Con and Mus and Sis know about the Attic Office. Made a vow, keep it close.

Between friends. Family.

Must have been some storage room, or insulation or whatever. We call it the Attic Office on account of the big desk sits there, legs all swollen with damp like old folks'. Back in the day, before the older kids started usin' the wrecks beneath it for their dirty business, me and Con used to play there. Con would sit behind the mouldy ol' desk and I'd come up them last few steps and I'd go *Knock knock?*

Come in says Con. I can hear him now. *What can I do for you today?*

Got any jobs?

Let me see. He glance down at imaginary papers on his desk. *Ah, yes, we have here a vacancy for a job as fireman—*

Cool. Cool.

But be quick! Run! Run! There's a fire started at

The Finger! Young lady need savin'!

Sis be lyin' across the room, placed herself underneath discarded mattress. *Aaaargh!* she yell. *The smoke! The flames!*

Don't just stand there, man I say to Con-Con. *Help me!*

And we throw the old three-legged chairs and wall panels aside, smash them and kick them, and all the while Sis screamin' *Help! Help!* And we have to carry her out to safety.

I laugh and I say *Got any jobs?* and Connor say *Yes, we got a dancin' vacancy.*

I can dance. I show some fancy moves. Con-Con say *Not that kind of dancin' – dancin' like this.* He show me his own freaky moves – like a skeleton doin' a waltz – and Sis come and breakdance. Three of us, struttin' through the debris, like a ecstasy of corpses.

Back in the day.

But the best bit I save all for myself. Not even Sis know about this. Sis think she Queen of the World, perchin' herself on her balcony ledge like she on mountaintops. Ain't nothin' compared to this.

I stomp through the wreckage. See sad loser's used works. Pathetic druggie found our Attic Office, been injectin'. Blood stains on beddin'.

No matter. I clamber on top of the desk, push my arms up. Up. Reach for a rectangular hatch like you get if you goin' up into a loft. But this ain't no loft.

This is the sky.

Soon as I push the hatch over on its hinge, the wind whooshin' at me. Howlin' like rage.

I always think to myself, if The Finger got a voice, this is it. I pull myself up. Climb through to another world. Wind whips around my head, like The Finger in foulest mood today. Even when it bright and sunny down on the ground, The Finger always ragin' a gale up top. I'm with it. Huffin' and puffin' up into a stormin' temper. The tempest.

On the roof, I'm crawlin' on my hands and knees, so's I don' get blown away. Like I'm lookin' for lost coins. Crawl to the middle, wind roarin' in my ears. It ain't got no secret to share with me. No *Who?* or *Why?* or *What?* demand the wind. Just one word, whole lungful of it. Yell it over and over, louder than the world.

No no no no no no no no no no no no no no no no no no no no no no no no no!

This is me. Deepest tempest of all.

I lie on my back. There ain't nothin' but concrete beneath me, cloud above. Honest sky. Nothin' but Heaven. The Finger is beneath me now. Every beef, every grief, every punch, kick, battle, all blasted clean away by the wind.

No suspension.

No shamin' Mum.

No missin' Dad.

No cheatin', scroungin', name-callin'.

No meat men.

No Finger, with no suckin' bugs. No bullet-hole poo. No crawlin' out your ear. No battle.

Marsh, are you involved with dealers?

No.

Floatin' through the clouds.

A Conversation I Have
Set to Memory

Beginnin' of summer I gave my brother a lesson in self-defence. Mum found out, threatened to throw me out the house. On account of Dad.

Like I said, I ain't gettin' with kids runnin' with gangs, carryin' blades, taxin' other kids or whatever. It's a fool's game. But Con-Con, he only a little kid, as likely get taxed as any others.

See, someone come at you with a blade, you need the knowledge to disarm them.

Mum say don' fight. Mum say give the fools what they askin', walk away. What Mum don' get is that you can never walk away.

You walk away one time, they gon' get you a second time.

You walk away the second time, they gon' get you a third.

Disarm them once, with efficiency, they gon' leave you be.

So how do you go about disarmin' a kid with a blade when you ain't carryin' one yourself?

<u>Self-Defence Technique Number One:</u> you <u>kick</u> the

knife out of their hand. Sweet. But remember, you gotta be enough distance from them get your angle right, and out of stab reach. Geometrics, right?

Self-Defence Technique Number Two: grab the wrist, twist the arm round the back. This a riskier strategy.

Same goes for Number Three: throw your mobile in their face – impressive results but not healthy for your phone.

Number Four: we won't even go into.

That day I was teachin' my brother Self-Defence Technique Number One: The Kick. My boy got a fine kick. Problem is, he ain't so keen on utilizin' the power he born with. Con-Con would rather turn tail, run as fast as you can. This itself is a successful technique, but only has short-term impact. Fools goin' to come back at you nex' day, and the day after.

Day gonna come when you ain't nowhere to run.

It got to be The Kick.

We in the livin' room experiencin' this lesson. Sabretooth shut out on the balcony on account of usin' Mum's knife from the kitchen – only a knife for butterin' toast, no deadliness. In practice it better to be hundred per cent authentical – so you get no unexpected surprises in the reality. But blunt knife probably wiser when practisin' with little brothers.

What happen? Mum comes home early.

She is far from impressed.

The reason my dad was sent to prison was because

he killed a man. I suppose this is why he in prison such a long time. He jailed for <u>manslaughter</u>. He not jailed for <u>murder</u> on account of him actin' in self-defence.

Dad put into action a technique that involved takin' the fool's knife and turnin' it on the fool. Fool died. Because of that, I been growin' up without no dad. Because of that, Mum in permanent stress.

But what if Dad hadn't taken the fool's knife? Dad would be the dead one. You want to live, you got to fight.

Mum flip.

Con say *We only playin' a game.*

Mum send him out on the balcony, join the dog.

She say I'm as bad as Dad.

I say *Dad ain't bad. I'm watchin' over Con-Con 'cos Dad ain't here.*

She say why do I think Dad not here?

I say *I don' know on account of he never writes to tell us about it.*

She say why do I think that is?

I kick over the coffee table.

That's the way she say, *the way of a man who teaches knife-fightin'.*

I wasn't teachin' knife-fightin'! I was teachin' how to fight knives! Be safe from the gangs.

She say she ever catch me teachin' Con-Con to fight again, she kick me out.

I say *Kick me out where? Out with the fools*

flashin' their blades. See me stabbed in the street?

She send me to my room.

She sit alone in the livin' room. I hear her sobbin'.

It is a conversation I have set to memory.

Don't Move an Inch

The wind blows memories roun' and roun' my head.

After a while, my head clear again. Brains been washed clean.

I climb back down through the hatch. I'm done feelin' sorry for myself. What we need right now is a plan.

Mum and Big Auntie can go see the council men if they like, it don't mean nothin'. *We got a infestation,* she gon' say, and the council men say *Ooh, we'll send round the pest men in a few weeks.* Only in a few weeks they ain't gon' be none of us left on account of we all been slurped up by them Dozen-Eggs-a-Day Megabugs, and they gonna be so starvatious they eat up all the pest men before they can even fill out their form. So thirsty they suck the ink outta the pest men's biros and the tears from their eyeballs.

We got to act now.

So here's me hammerin' on Mustaph's door, hopin' he ain't also been taken in the night. Door opens and his dad let me in with the usual cheery greetin' – not. I take this to be a good sign on account of his dad's big fat belly. If I was a hungry bug I would give myself a big proper feast on Mustaph's dad before goin' onto the leaner pickin's. Mustaph skinny, like prison-camp skinny, just a bag of bones in scabby jeans that only be stayin' up 'cos Mus keepin' a tight hold of them all the time. When he doin' his sprayin', he tuck the spray cans into the waist, otherwise he'd be creatin' his art with his strides round his ankles, and it wouldn't be no vandalism he'd be gettin' lifted for, but exposure. I asked him once why he ain't got no belt and he say he do have a belt. I asked him why he don't wear it, and he looked at me like I was crazy. *Who wears belts?* he said.

Mus? I say, and push open the door to his den. I am hit with a faceful of pongy body smell, which is the usual state of affairs.

Can't see nothin' 'cos of the drawn curtains, but I can hear a steady breathin'. <u>In out.</u> <u>In out.</u> Lazy dog mus' be nappin' still.

Mus?

I remind myself always bring a lighter when you come into this space, 'cos you can never see even the tip of your own nose.

<u>Pitter-pat.</u>

I freeze when I hear that. Flex my legs and wave my arms all aroun' me like I be the Kung Fu expert and my invisible foes about to be karate-jabbed to a pulp. Touch nothin'. Listen. Listen hard.

Mus?

In the darkness, somethin' press against the tip of my nose. I yell and punch in wild panic into the blackness. Nothin'.

Mus?

Something tickle the back of my neck. A Mega leg. I swing round and punch wildly. Nex' thing, I'm blinded by a beam of light, a shadowy figure behind it, goggles, heavy breath. A hand lift up the goggles and I see Mustaph's ugly mug grinnin' at me.

Boo.

I nearly smack him. *What you doin', bro? You scarin' the bones offa me, man!*

I pull open his curtains, which is breakin' the only rule Mustapha ever set, but I'm too mad to care. Mustaph standin' there like some kind of space engineer, holdin' onto his big torch and with ridiculous big goggles in his hands.

My new toy he say, like that explain everythin'.

I snatch the goggles. They weigh a ton. *What's these?*

He's well pleased with himself, breakin' a rare grin. *Night vision.*

What? Man, for what you be needin' a pair of night-vision goggles?

He just shrug. *I wanted to see.*

See what?

The bugs, of course. The giant ones.

Damn, my boy is a genius. *Did you see any?*

He shrug again, strolls over and places them night

goggles on his bust of Beethoven like that where they naturally belong.

Shoulda seen yo' face in the dark he say, reachin' down to wrap his duvet up over his pencil-thin shoulders. *So. Wassup?* Like he ain't even heard the sirens or nothin', lost in Mustaphaland.

I look around. He ain't got no bullet holes in his walls.

When I tell him about seein' the meat wagons carryin' out Sleepy Lady he jus' nod his head like I tol' him I'm goin' to watch the football on downstairs's widescreen.

I say *All these dead bodies that be gettin' carried out regular as puttin' out the rubbish – they all been sucked dry by the monster bugs.*

Oh yeah Mus say, like I told him Man United beat Chelsea 2–1.

They come and suck you dry when you be asleep I say.

Right he answer me.

I see I got to prod this boy awake with a big stick. *Like vampires.*

Finally he got a serious look on his face. I ain't sure whether it's 'cos he shocked about the killings or excited 'cos I mentioned vampires. With Mus you jus' can't tell.

So we gon' get ourselves some weaponry and we gon' kill ourselves one of these Megabugs and then people believe. Then we get a crew together and we gon' have ourselves a Bug War, yeah?

OK he say. Jus' like that.

We go knock-knockin' on Sis's door. Grab my dog on the way up. Big Auntie already upped sticks for a VIP Pow-Wow with the council men.

Sis say *Big Auntie been talkin' to the police about what she callin' <u>contaminated heroin</u>. She reckon <u>dirty smack</u> hittin' the street and causin' everybody to die like livin' goin' out of fashion.*

She give us a moment to absorb this news, and she fix me with her big warm eyes and say *So, boys, caught any big ones yet?*

They didn't show, did they? 'Cos they knew I was sittin' there waitin' to bust their bubbles with Mum's fryin' pan. They feasted on Sleepy Lady instead. You see them body-baggin' her out?

Mus jus' shrug and stroll out onto the balcony.

Sis nod. I know she considerin' whether or not she believe me. Everybody else in the whole world say I got myself <u>behavioural issues</u>. Just another way of sayin' I'm a nutjob. Sis don't wanna be thinkin' I'm no nutjob. She know what it's like 'cos she been called worse in her time. She be thinkin' it's us what are the sane ones, rest of the world gone bonkers. Sis got an easy face to read, like Mustaph in that respect. Some days I look at them havin' a whole conversation with each other, without sayin' a word, jus' their eyes passin' vibes back and forth between each other like weird invisible tennis. Me, my mouth do all my talkin' for me, and an excellent job it do of it – true.

Mustaph already stood stretched out on the balcony wall, doin' his mornin' greetin' to the world, jus' like Sis do. She hop up and join him, like that there wall be jus' four feet off of the groun', rather than four hundred feet. They standin' tall, arms stretched to the clouds like Spider-Man and Spider-Lady 'bout to perform a show.

Wooo-hoooh! go Sis, to the heavens.

Wooo-hoooh! Mus answer her like little wolf brother. It make me dizzy jus' watchin' 'em.

I'm boilin' up. If Mum had of believed me, maybe we could have saved Sleepy Lady. She didn't have to die in the night, blood sucked by some vampire bug, get carted off in the wrong type of sleepin' bag. If Compo had listened, maybe we could have saved Mr Bush too. Most important of all, we could have done somethin' for them poor kids. I'm sick. I turn away. I see somethin' make my blood freeze.

Don't move I mutter.

Ain't goin' nowhere Sis answer. *Jus' enjoyin' my mornin' stretch, oh yeah.*

I'm serious I say. *Don't move an inch.*

Straightaways, the two of 'em turn round and set their eyes right where my peepers be set. There be one evil monster starin' straight back at us.

It's perched there on the wall above Sis's window, only a few feet away. Even though I been lookin' for one of these suckers all night long, it still make me break into a sweat like a snowman in a heatwave.

Sis cooler than that. She break into a big, knowin' grin and nod *Ah-haaa* like it be jus' the confirmation she expectin'. *Well, you is certainly correct, isn't you, Marshall the First?*

We blink at the bug and it stare back at us, unflinchin'. Red-eyed.

Mustaph lookin' at it all serene, like it some pretty butterfly landed on his hand.

I feel relief.

You think it gonna pounce? asks Sis.

No I answer. *That what I'm sayin'. They is sneaky. Wait until you sleepy, then suck you nice and easy.*

Sis shivers. *What we gon' do?*

Go get yo' fry pan. Slow and smooth. Don' scare it off. If it creep close enough, we splatter it, yeah?

I was right. I am not a nutjob. I am a sane boy. Other people see it now, with their own eyes. That be three of us. Soon it be a lot more.

Mum and my social worker and Subo, the fat Maths teacher, might figure I got me anger issues, but right about now, I'm sweet with that. If that sucker come near me, I will rip off its head.

Sis come back with a fryin' pan, a carvin' knife and a broom.

Bug watches us. It got two bug eyes stickin' outta the side of its head, unblinkin', like blobs of blood. Proboscis like Satan's snout. Antennas twitchin' away, like it knows for sure we there. Spiky brown hairs comin' outta its side, in need of a good shave. Big, flat, brown, stripy body. <u>Flat.</u> Even now I know enough that it in need of feedin'. Its body kinda transluscent, so's you can see it ain't got no blood in it. Just a empty sachet, waitin' to be filled up. Ain't movin' a inch. Six legs taut against the rough concrete – ready to run, or pounce. Vibin' us out.

Outta the corner of my eye, I see another sucker, down by the side of the window. I nudge Sis. We say nothin', but roll our eyes roun', and there be another one, down the other side.

Three of 'em. Bugs like to hide out durin' the day – that's why we ain't been seein' 'em – but this mob mus' be gettin' hungry. Or greedy.

What we gon' do? ask Sis.

What we gon' do? We gon' do what you always gon' do when you got three ugly bugs on all sides givin' you the evils. We gon' attack.

Mustaph the tallest, and Sis hand him the broom. I tool myself up with the fry pan.

Sis and Mus don' say a word. She gesturin' with her eyes, one, two, three, from one of the Megas to the next, then at the end of Mustaph's broom. They doin' their silent talkin'. It clear in my mind that Sis want Mus to knock these suckers off of their perches in quick succession. She look to me and then at Bug Number One, like it my job to squish it when it drop. Then she point her thumb at her chest and look up to Bug Number Two. She give the evil eye to Bug Number Three, and raise her eyebrows at Mus. A team, see?

Mus gonna knock 'em down one at a time. I get to smash the first one. Lickin' my lips with the anticipation.

Sabretooth whinin' and trottin' on the spot like he awaitin' instruction of his own. I put the flat of my hand to his direction. Clever dog know that mean he got to be still.

Bugs still be vibin' us out, like they waitin' to see what we gon' do. Me and Sis waitin' for Mustaph to make his move. Mustaph give a silent sigh. You can see all his muscles relaxin' and his breathin slowin' almost to a halt. Me, I broken into a nasty sweat, heart hammerin' inside my chest like it want to be let the hell out of there. Sis narrows her eyes like she psychin' herself into a state of maximum aggression.

Bam! Mustaph swing the broom faster than a bolt of lightnin'. Whack! Right on the back of Bug Number One. For a moment that bug don't do nothin', jus' flinch a bit. Out the corner of my eye, his two crew take off faster than a pair of bag-snatchers. Bam! Mustaph strike Bug Number One again, just as it turnin' to run away. Down it come, waftin', like a sheet of paper, slow but fast. Mus step back so I got space to smash it with the fry pan, but is tricky to tell where it gonna land.

Sabe pounces forward, teeth bared and hackles

high, right under my feet. Bug hit the floor and
Sabreboy be snappin' in its general direction. I bend
over my dog and strike with the fry pan, but the bug
done move the second its legs hit the ground. <u>Clang!</u>
The fry pan connects with concrete, jarrin' my wrist
and bendin' in two like a pranged car bonnet. Flame
of pain leap up my arm. Cuss it. Sis leap forward,
slicin' the air with her carver, lickety-split quick as
the bug. Bug got a head start and scurryin' straight
back up the wall. Out of arm's reach, it turns round.
I swear, it stops and stares at us. Its antennas
quiverin' in the air, like it takin' time to take note of
our smell. Red eyes on either side of its mug fix first
on Sis, then on Mustaph, then on me.

Sabretooth does a wee on the floor.

Satisfied with itself, the bug swaggers off up
the wall.

Well, well, well say Sis. *See what we got here.* She
bend down and pick somethin' from the ground.

It's about eighteen inches long. A schnozzle,
severed from the point where it joined the bug head.
Sucker ain't got no sucker no more. Sis hold it up in
one hand, her knife in the other, pride on her face.
She's my Sister Rambo.

Looks like we got ourselves the evidence we after.

Forensics

Sabre havin' a good sniff and a lick, like he tryin' to absorb clues as to what ingredients make up a giant bedbug proboscis. Look to me like it ain't so tasty. Schnozzle is reddish brown, razor sharp at the tip, for stabbin' through your skin. I figure that help them bugs dig good and deep on whatever tragic soul it is they slurpin' from.

Sis pick it up by the end and jab the air with it like a cutlass. *Yargh!* she go, like a mental pirate. *Yargh!*

Stop it, Sis.

She peer into the end of it. *All hollow. Guess it just a giant blood-straw.* She sniff it, wrinkle her nose. *Smell worse than school dinner.*

I take it off her, have a sniff myself. Sis is right. It smells like stewed bones. Makes me shiver.

Mustaph grab it from me, take a sniff also. He breaks into a big smile. *Oh, yummy yoo.*

My friends are too sick. *So what we gonna do?*

Sis smile. *Like you say. Evidence, yeah? Let's go present it to Big Auntie.*

Sis always refer to her mum as Big Auntie, like <u>Big</u>

<u>Auntie</u> be the name printed on her birth certificate.

I have a realization. <u>Mum.</u> Finally, she goin' to have to believe me. She'll stop suspectin' me, say sorry good and proper. Makes me feel all light, after the fierceness of our bullet-hole battle.

Big Auntie ain't back yet from Pow-Wowin' with the authorities. She oughta be back. We need her here in The Finger, see our evidence, form a plan. So we go through her flat, head towards ours, see if Mum be there.

But as we makin' our way down the stairwell, who do we come face to face with but oinkboy Compo – with two uniformed coppers and a inspector sportin' a genuine detective overcoat.

Compo got one of them faces like a dented shovel. Nose pokin' at you and chin juttin' out like a muddied blade. Nothin' he like more than diggin' the dirt, yeah? *Well, well.* He turn towards overcoat man like he's his best buddy. *Talk of the devils. You want to know about drug-dealing and similar, these are the youth for interrogating.*

I'm feelin' my fists bunchin' up even as he speaks. Sabretooth curlin' his lip, givin' a low growl, like I taught him when Compo in the vicinity. *Sit, boy* I say.

Hiyah! Sis is flashin' these fellas her cheesiest beam, but I ain't havin' none of it.

Yo, Compo. You know we ain't got nothin' to do with that rubbish. Never have. What you wantin' to spread lies for?

Compo and the real police are right in our faces, inspectin' us like we is just a infestation ourselves. Compo turn to one of the uniforms and mutter *Like father, like son*. Uniform nod his head in agreement.

Shouldn't you all be in school? asks overcoat cop, all cool like he thinkin' he Inspector Morse.

Sis give him her big smile. *Permanent exclusion, yeah?*

I fold my arms. *Temporary suspension, yeah?*

Mustaph just stand there and grin like a idiot.

Compo take a step forward. *I say we take 'em in.*

Uniform cop got his hand on his utilities, like he just itchin' for some baton action. Man in charge look less certain. Suppose that's why he in charge. Imagine if a fool like Compo make all the big decisions. You have riotin' breakin' out on every street corner.

Inspector Morse say *I hear you young people were among the last to be seen with the ... deceased.*

Sis roll her eyes.

That's right Compo urges. *Let's nick 'em.*

Inspector Morse squintin' at our faces, inspectin' our eyeballs, seein' if we on drugs or not. Problem with Muskrat is he got them sort of eyes always look blissed out anyways. But Sis step up. *We heard about them little kids. We ain't been doin' nothin' but tryin' to find out what goin' on ourselves.*

She straighten her face so she got the look of a good-standin' citizen, type that collect sponsors for charity runs for the aged.

Anyway we can help? Mus jut his lower jaw out, which is what he do the two times a year he tryin' to show enthusiasm. It make him look like he needin' the loo.

As it happens says Comp, steppin' forward.

Leave them be says Morse. *They're just kids. If we need to, we can ask them questions later.*

OK say Comp. *Come on, I'll lead you to the victims' places of abode.*

<u>Places of abode.</u> If only Comp knew what a jerk he sounded.

But Inspector Morse lingerin', givin' us the once over.

Listen he say. *You kids discover anything useful, you let us know. Anything that might help.* He offers a smile and starts to turn, but stops and adds *Take care of yourselves.*

Come say Sis, *let us take our evidence to Big Auntie. She got first dabs on this.*

As we make our way further down, we hear footsteps clompin' behind us. We stop and turn. Nex' moment, Compo dash down round the corner, on his own. He step up to us, lookin' straight at me, as if he jus' remembered he had somethin' to tell.

He gone and changed his face, try and relax out the bully-frowns. Open his mouth, but don' quite know what to say. I get it. He so determined to get results, impress his hero Inspector Morse, that he prepared to change tactic.

We could all work to resolve this together, you know.

I snort.

He lookin' at me like he ... pity me. He put his hands in his pockets, tryin' hard as he can to relax his body language, like he been taught on some Community Relations seminar. Look of pity on his face deepens. I'm feelin' my fists clenchin' up. <u>Don't you look at me like that.</u>

Kids... He tries a smile. *We know you love your community...*

Man is a joke.

We know you are loyal to your neighbours...

Maybe I oughta give Sabretooth the nod. Give Compo's ankles a bit of a nip.

But some of these neighbours of yours, well, we've seen the result of their work up close, haven't we? Not very neighbourly at all. Deadly concoctions being peddled on the corner. Marshall... He give me his softest look. *I know you're close to these people. You have loyalty—*

Yeah, I do. Findin' myself squarin' up to him.

He says *I was talking to your mother last night—*

Don't I say, my arm reachin' roun' behind my back.

She's worried about you.

Don't you dare.

He places his hand on my shoulder. *I'm—*

I jerk my arm out from behind my back, bug proboscis gripped in my fist. I jab the razor point towards his big fat gut.

You don't talk to my mother!

I wave the schnozzle beneath his piggie chin. *We can sort out our own problems, yeah? And see this, this is our proof, all we need. When my mum sees this...*

Compo look down at the proboscis.

Sabretooth curl his lip, give a low snarl.

I see Sis out the corner of my eye, puttin' a calmin' palm towards my dog. She know better than to try and calm me the same way.

Compo lift his gaze, meet my eyes. He looks sad for me, and I hate him. I feel his fingers curlin' round the shaft of the proboscis, him takin' it, smooth, out of my grip. My fingers let him.

Temper, temper he whispers.

He take a step back.

I crouch down, put my hands round my dog's neck, ruffle his fur. Let him lick at my fingers. It's all I can do.

Compo look at what he got in his hand, and the old sly look return to his eyes. *This is an offensive weapon.* He shakes his head, slow, sarcastic.

Sis sighs deeply. *It's—*

Don't worry. He waves his hand dismissively. Then his eyes start seein' it properly. *What is it?*

It's—

Looks like some kind of a... he begins, but he can't finish a sentence that goin' to end as stupidly as ... *the schnozzle of a giant bug.* Instead, a sneer creeps across his face and he says *Looks like some kind of a … pipe?* He loves that. *Drugs paraphernalia. You're carrying a bong.*

Muskrat sniggers and rolls his eyes. He almos' can't contain his laughter, thinkin' of them uniform boys back at the station, passin' that proboscis round in a circle, inhalin' like fools tryin' to get a high.

I ain't laughin'. Pet my dog. Let him lick every finger.

I could have you all brought in for this says Compo.

But Sis ain't havin' none of that. *You been lookin' for evidence about all of them ODs, yeah? Bet you ain't found nothin' in Mr Bush' flat, or at Sleepy – that skinny ol' lady's place?* She flash her twinkly smile at our local Police Community Support Officer. *Well, we jus' found this, down on the stairwell. Reckon it add to the evidence you need, yeah?*

Genius Sis. She know as well as me that we go blabbin' all about giant bugs crawlin' up the walls, they gonna be thinkin' we on drugs for sure. Lock us up straight away. Instead, let Comp and his cronies figure things out on their ownsome.

He thinkin' this over. *OK* he say. *I'll keep it. This is probably a … vessel, yes, a vessel for the contaminated drugs. My colleagues will be very interested in this. Give it to forensics.*

That pleases him. <u>Forensics.</u> Proper police word. He rolls it round his mouth.

Muskrat give him a snarky salute.

Comp ignores my fool friend, looks back at me. *You keep out of trouble.*

He marches off, jackboots clip-cloppin' along the stairway with self-importance.

I turn to Sis. *Sweet.*

Only problem she say, *is he just walked away with our evidence. I never even got chance to take a pic. How we gonna prove things to Big Auntie now?*

Or Mum.

Rubbish

Sis don't have nothin' to say to me on the way up
to hers.

Then, once we all sat down, comfy on cushions on
her rug, cup of tea in our hands, she says *You out of
control, Marshall.*

This is what my mum would say. I don't answer.

*Compo could have had you charged, threatenin'
him like that. You be locked up for a long time. That
what you want?*

Exactly like my mum.

Take us down with you, the way you was behavin'.

I'm ticklin' my dog, space between his ears. He
like that.

Muskrat look like he listenin' intently. Hard to tell.

She goes on. *Thought we was plannin' on how to
take down these bugs? Get folk to start believin' us?*

Sabes got his muzzle restin' on my legs, chillin'. I
shrug. She shrug back. She is well mad at me.

It's your temper, innit? she say. *Well out of order.*

I ain't risin' to that. *Come* I say to my dog, standin'
up, *let's go.*

Muskrat comes right out of his trance. *Where you goin'?*

Like you care.

From where she is lyin', Sis hooks her foot around the back of my ankle. She ain't meanin' to trip me, but if I want to take a step I gotta lift my foot over hers. I can feel her toes through her socks, brushin' against the back of my ankle, soft.

Marsh?

I'm not goin' to cry. Need to turn my face.

Sis shifts her gaze down to the rug, breathes for a few seconds. I don't know what to do. She starts talkin'. *All of us got issues, ain't we?* She rubbin' her toes against my heel, like it's a hand restin' on my shoulder. *Like me, I didn't believe you about the giant bugs. I'm sorry, I shoulda believed you. You're my friend. Act like a cage wrestler half the time, but it ain't jus' temper, Marsh. You know that. 'Cos even though nobody believed you, you still carried on, try and do somethin' about the bugs.*

I believed him says Mustaph.

She ignores him. *That's courage, boy. We got dead folk bein' carried out from all up The Finger. Anybody get saved, they goin' to be saved because of you. You guarded Connor, yeah?* I can feel my knuckle-dust rage tricklin' down towards my feet. *If the rest of us goin' to keep livin', we need you too. So don' go gettin' all mad and stormin' out.* She splays her fingers out, across the fluffiness of the rug. *You're bigger than that.*

I don' know what to do. Can't think. My mind feel like the empty space on the wall, where my dad's picture used to be.

She smile up at me. *Chill, boy. Sit.*

Sabreboy think she givin' him an instruction, settles back down. I copy my dog.

So we sit in silence for a while, drinkin' our tea, thinkin' about how things are. No sound 'cept Mustaph blowin' on his tea once in a while, tryin' to cool it down.

Finally Sis says *OK, we all seen the giant bugs, we convinced. Now, we got to convince others, Big Auntie and your mum espesh. We handed over our only evidence* – she hurries on, before I can react – *but that's a good thing. Police will be able to confirm what we up against – eventually. Once the authorities get involved, things will change. Meanwhile, we on our own. I been sendin' messages to some of the young ones roundabout. They can generate whole heap of gossip, get folks geed up. But when night comes, whole of The Finger goin' to come under bug attack, 'less we come up with the goods. So, what else we got?*

Mustaph slowly raises his forefinger, like he in Year 3 and Sis the teacher.

Yes?

They hidin', ain't they.

Man, my dog can come up with better than that.

Me and Sis both cross our arms, stare at him.

Them bugs hide in the spines of books, don' they? And behind posters and 'neath mattresses.

That's it?

Sis says *That's the little bugs, Musky. We know where <u>they</u> are. It's the big ones we got to find. And a way to destroy 'em.*

'Zackly. He's lookin' all pleased with himself. *So the first step is to find them, yeah?*

This goin' to be a long plannin' session.

He goes on. *Been a hot summer, yeah?* We noddin' our heads, geein' him to the point. *Sis, what you say happen to the bugs in the hot weather?*

She lean forward. *They breed more regular. Their eggs hatch more quickly. They grow much bigger.*

'Zackly he say again. *And they hide in the dark.*

Sis land her fists on his knees, all urgent. *Mus, do you know where the Megabugs are hidin' out?*

Maybe he say. *But findin' out goin' to be a highly dangerous mission.*

Now both me and Sis much more animated. *Where are they, Mus?*

Well, see he says, *the rubbish chute has been blocked for months—*

The rubbish chute! Connects to every floor, stinks so bad no one'll go near it. And dark. Very, very dark.

You're a genius.

What do we do?

Well he sips his tea, which is now the required

temperature, and lays out his masterplan. *We need my night-vision goggles, boilersuit, Sabretooth's extendible dog leash, can of Doktor Doom, and one more thing.*

Mustaph's plans are like jabbin' forks into a plugged-in toaster.

What's that, Mus?

A volunteer.

Safer Neighbourhood Team

You're crazy say Sis. *For starters, your dog lead ain't goin' to stretch all the twenty floors down The Finger.*

Mus give me a look like to say that Sis the biggest simpleton in the world.

We don' do it from the <u>top</u>, of course. Second-floor chute flap been broken for months. Just a gapin' hole. We go from there.

Even so say Sis, *Sabretooth's lead ain't gon' take Marshall's weight. Snap within two seconds.*

Ah Mus replies, *it's special strong cable, yeah? They make these things to pull back big Rottweilers and Alsations and other such beasts.*

She shakin' her head. *It's a crazy idea. Too dangerous.*

We makin' our way down to the second floor. Sis is wrong. Sabe's lead <u>will</u> hold, it's seven metres long, and it got a break button and a lock, even a retractable control. True, that won't retract me all the way back up, but I can jus' hang on while they haul me. I'm more worried about the Megas. We goin' to spray me down with Doktor Doom, put those critters off to begin with, and I'll have a can to squirt in their faces if they get too close. But I'm also takin' the knife that Sis used to cut off the first Mega's snout.

In any case, I'll only be down there for a few seconds. Jus' long enough take a picture of 'em, use as evidence, then I'm straight back up.

Nothin' can go wrong say Mustaph. And he the originator of the plan.

Why me? Why me be the volunteer go down and pull this stunt?

First up, Mustaph begs off, sayin' it's his idea, so that's his bit done. Ain't sure about his logic there, but let it go. I got a feelin' if we lowered Mustaph down into the pits of the bug shaft, we might never see him again. Not with blood still flowin' through him anyway.

And Sis? I jus' can't let her. We argue about it for a while. She don't want me thinkin' she scared of doin' her bit. But it's me – I started this battle, and so far I done nothin' but jinx it up.

Who died already?

Soft Stuart.

Sleepy Lady.

Someone whose face we don' see.

Mr Bush.

Someone else whose face we don' see.

The littl'uns, Leo and Lola.

That's seven Empties.

How many more we don' know about yet?

And Sis get the evidence we need to stop this thing, what do I do? I give it to Compo. Man, I deserve to get locked up. I'm a First-Class Loser.

I started this fight. I put all the others at risk. Now it my job to finish it.

Duty.

We stop off at Mustaph's where he got a old orange boilersuit he used for some crazy project. We give it a thorough sprayin' with Doktor Doom, and I put it on. Then I put on the night-vision goggles.

You look like one of them captured terrorists, 'bout to be dragged into a torture room say Sis. *I don' like it. How do we know they ain't goin' to leap on you, chew you right up?*

Come on, Sis, chill. You read all that stuff on Wikipedia. They don' pounce. They wait until you is asleep, then <u>creep up on you</u>. *These buglies are cowards. Anyway, we don' know for sure they goin' to be down there.*

Mus is with me on this. *They sneaks, ain't they? Night sneaks. Hence the windows.*

What windows? me and Sis say at the same time.

Windows. He shrug. *That how they go about their business. Why they thrivin' in this hot weather. On account of we all leave our windows open.* He sighs. *You two in need of a education.* He turns to me. *Marsh, when you saw their scatterin' of bullet-hole poo, what was it nex' to?*

The window. Boy got a point. The Megas get at us by comin' in and out of our windows. Just wish he wasn't lookin' at us like we was idiots. Comin' from Muskrat, it a insult. Then I think, I spent all night tryin' to stay awake, shinin' my torch round all my cupboards and beneath the beds, and all I needed to have done was <u>shut the windows</u>. Musk is right. Pass me the dunce's hat.

These guys is lazy says Musk, all confident. *They don' want no battle. Trust me.*

Here we be, standin' by the rubbish chute, second floor of The Finger, me with goggles, orange boilersuit, belt round my waist with a dog lead attached to it, my loyal crew at the other end of the lead.

Sabreboy starin' at me, wonderin' why the wrong one of us is on the end of the leash. <u>What?</u> <u>They takin' Marshall for walkies?</u>

Me and Mus playin' tug-o'-war with the cable, jus' to prove how antisnappable it is. Mus ain't got no chance in a game of tug, on account of his scrawniness. I pull him over, but Mus bein' Mus he ain't lettin' go of his end, and he make me reel him in like he a big fish and I Angler of the Year.

Sis gets a strop on, says we gotta get ourselves organized.

We take our positions. Sis got the plastic handle of the lead slipped round her own belt, Mustaph got his arms wrapped round her waist, his hips diggin' up against her bottom, like a couple of naughty doggies. Compo walk round the corner right now, ain't none of us goin' to live it down.

Boilersuit equipped with multiple pockets, so I got my mobile close to hand, as well as the Doktor Doom. As the man said *What could possibly go wrong?*

Two of them lift me feet first, face down into the gapin' hole in the wall, look like someone done a job on a cash machine with a JCB. Stink comin' up from the shaft so bad, no one could tell whether it be a giant bug den or jus' months' worth of tower-block crap. If I'm really unlucky, it be both.

Sabre is trottin' up and down on the spot, whinin', agitated. This <u>way</u> outta his comfort zone.

I shuggle my legs and my waist over the lip of the shaft, rest there on my elbows a moment, before I begin my abseil.

Goodbye to bad rubbish says Mustaph. He ain't even funny.

Black walls covered in slime. As I lower myself, look up, the hole I crawled through is a white square of light. I think it is the light at the end of the tunnel, and I am travelling away from it. Smell my own terror sweat, addin' to the ripe mix assaultin' my nose.

Slime coverin' the walls is actually <u>green</u>. No, it isn't. Mustapha's dumb goggles makin' everythin' look green. I inch my way down, soles of my trainers against the wall of the shaft, keep my balance, like

I'm mountaineerin' into Hell.

Look up. White square of light shrunk down so it look no bigger than a letter box. Remind me of Mr B's letter box, but now I'm on the same side of it as the bugs.

Leapin'. Leapin' right at my face.

Get a grip. I can hear my own panic, breathin' its echo round and round me. Reach for my knife – jus' checkin', jus' checkin' – throw my balance out, feet slip on the slime, whole body twizzle round the leash, my back thuddin' against the side of the shaft. *Ooph!*

(Ooph!) go my echo.

Y'all right down there?

(...'own there?)

Voice from a mile away. Earth callin' Marshall?

Marsh?

(...'arsh?)

Un-huh.

(...uh.)

I give 'em a thumbs up, forgettin' they can't see jack.

This is stupidity.

Pitter-pat.

No, no. Tell me I didn't hear that. Jus' my feet gettin' a grip back on the wall, is all.

Pitter-pat.

Jus' my trainers, is all.

Bend my head. Focus on the bottom of the shaft. Can't make much out. Shapes. Junk?

I hear a _ping_!

High above. A _clump_. A—

Oh shit!

(...'_hit!_)

I'm fallin', droppin' to the bottom of the pit.

Twist myself roun' jus' before I hit the bottom.

Green vision plummetin' up at my goggles.
Scrunch into somethin' soft and brittle. _Snap_, _crackle_
and _pop_! Blackness. Whole body swallowed up.
Buzzin' in my ears.

Gasp. Insects shootin' into my mouth. Fillin' my
nose. Scream. Hear no scream, only buzzin'. No air.
No breath.

My head pullin' itself up. Up. Feet paddin' for
solid ground, snappin' twigs? Brushin' old carpet.
Stickiness. Upright. Filth slidin' off of me.

Putrid. I puke. Odour of decay. Keep pukin'.

Chokin'. Spittin'. Goo all over my hands.

Shakin' my head. Clear my ears. _Buzz buzz buzz._

Rotten stench. Pukin', pukin' up a foulness.

Eyes open. Open wide. Look. Look, see.

Waist-deep in a swamp of old furniture, rugs,
snapped twigs.

Hold out my hands. Green. I see. Intestines?

Look down. Dog skull grinnin' up at me.

Not rugs.

Cat fur, smeared in grease.

Claw and fang scattered like confetti among

rotten, swollen animal hide. Hair of dog and cat, floatin' like dust.

Not bugs. A swarm of flies tryin' to get into my head. And maggots, everywhere.

This is a animal abbatoir.

Now I'm screamin'.

Mustaph was <u>so</u> wrong.

I scream like a maniac. Scream like a baby.

Zillion flies, dartin' and buzzin' roun' my head. Up my nose and in my ears.

Hearin' screamin' and yellin' from up above.

Stench like rotten meat and ancient cheese makin' me heave again. Ain't got nothin' left to chuck up. Start tryin' to climb the walls. Can't get a grip. Try and wedge myself, legs on one side of the wall, arms on the other. Fall, almost sink back into the decayin' pets. It look like some of them still alive. Squint down – no, is maggots squirmin'.

Oh, he was <u>so</u> wrong.

Scream some more and stop. Irritatin', waste of time.

No noise from up above. My friends deserted me.

I am sinkin' into a pile of dead dogs, gastric sludge, ruptured gut. Animal hair swirlin' all roun', gettin' up my nose, makin' me sneeze. Sneeze make me barf. Nothin' come, jus' my own fume, mix with odour of decay.

<u>Buzz buzz.</u>

A loud <u>CRACK</u> and daylight suddenly dazzlin' me. A dog bounds forward into the pit, fangs snappin'. My dog. As the tide of dead pets slide out onto the ground outside the shaft, Sabre yelps, turns tail and legs it. I remove my goggles. Sis standin' there holdin' a seriously hefty crowbar, lookin' ill with worry. Mustaph doin' a dodge-the-dead-dog-avalanche dance.

Stench hits them and they both sick.

Sis drop the crowbar. I stagger out. Go to her. She give me a rib-crunchin' hug. Over her shoulder I see Mustaph scratchin' his head, tryin' to work out how his masterplan went so wrong.

Leftovers

I'm wrigglin' out of the boilersuit fast as if I got maggots on the inside of it as well as the out. I feel infested. Suit covered in pet juice. Stink of dead man's clothes.

Thought you said the cord wouldn't snap? I yell at Mustaph.

It didn't he say. *The handle did.*

And what about the Megas? I'm ragin' at him. *You said the Megas were down here!*

Just a educated guess...

I leap at him. *Educated? You ain't even been in school all year. What make you think you can make a <u>educated</u> guess?*

I didn't get no sleep, did I? I was up all night. How can I think clever when I ain't had no sleep?

I ain't had no sleep either. Guess that why I listened to your genius idea.

OK, let's calm down a bit say Sis. *People beginnin' to stare.*

Like I care.

To be fair, it's myself I'm really mad at. I mean, I

listened to Mustaph. What kind of fool idea is that? Megas have instigated a serious feud and we takin' our lead from brains like Mustaph?

So here's me for all the neighbourhood to see, in nothin' more than my boxers and my trainers, ankle-deep in Fido and Tiddles's fur coats.

Sis and Mus can't hardly believe their eyes. They seein' a 57 variety of different breeds. Pit bulls to Jack Russells to moggies. We seein' dog fang and cat fang bared and fierce where the skin of the lips been stretched back by rot. Ginger cat flanks squeezed in next to doggie black and tan, skin and bone. A mass grave of family pets.

LOST DOG: Jimbob

Has Anybody Seen Romeo?

Reward Offered For Return of Missing Tinky

We been full-time fools. Thank God I always keep Sabretooth close by my side. These bugs been keepin' their diet nice and stable by chompin' on family pets, wait until they bred themselves into a massive enough posse before showin' to us humans. Once they sucked dry, bugs been draggin' the evidence to the rubbish chute, droppin' them in.

Least they throw their rubbish away when they done with it say Mus.

Sabre is highly aggravated, pawin' the ground and whinin', his nose twitchin' with a hundred horrible smells. I can see in his eyes he actually enraged. Never seen that in my dog before. His nose like he assessin' information when we walk by a lamppost, find out who been passin' by. I figure some of these were his friends. He'd of known some of them since he was a pup.

My dog raises his snout to the heavens, begins to howl.

We standin' with our heads down, lettin' Sabe have his moment.

They all dead? says Sis.

All dead.

Smashed-open hatch at the bottom of the chute looks like a cupboard been stuffed full to overflow, jus' waitin' for someone to open up. It been opened up all right.

Council goin' to think Finger folk surpassed ourselves this time, dumpin' all our dead pets down the rubbish chute. They gonna say we less than human, don' deserve decent places to live.

I'm oiking phlegm up my throat. I still got a maggot lodged in there, need to drink a gallon of water.

Clompin' the side of my head with the palm of my hand, tryin' to dislodge the last of the flies from my ears. Try and gouge them out with my little finger.

Come say Sis, *let's get you dressed. You look like you need a lie-down.*

Mustaph standin' fascinated by the pile of dead pets, dippin' his toe in, enjoyin' his curiosity.

Hey, brains Sis call him, *come on, we need to regroup.*

All of a sudden I feel woozy. Gotta go sit down on the kerb before I fall and bash my head. Sis send Mus for some water. *Quick as you can!*

He speed off. I stagger to the edge of the kerb, and me and Sis sit.

What I don' get say Sis after a moment, *is why there be dozens of dead pets down the rubbish chute.*

Come on, Sis, you ain't no fool.

She shiver. *This is where the Megas dump their leftovers.*

But they bright enough to make sure they hidin' out elsewhere. This ain't no help to us.

Suppose we show somebody? I mean, apart from people in The Finger. Take a dead dog to the council, or police?

They gonna slam the cuffs on us straight away. 'Member Cat Bin Lady?

Lady who chucked her cat in a wheelie bin? Was all over the Internet?

You fancy bein' the new Cat Bin Lady?

Mus back from the corner shop, break the world hundred metre record.

I grab the bottle of water. Down it.

Clear my throat, wash down the maggot stuck in my windpipe.

Maybe if we dig aroun', we can find some proper evidence? he say.

I grimace at Mustaph, nod at the pile of bodies. *Be my guest.*

Look say Sis, *I think one of them is still alive.*

Hate to tell you this, but that's jus' maggots wigglin' underneath the skin.

But Sis on her feet. *No. I can see its eyes movin'. Look.*

She is right. It is a little dog, Chiwowow, like WAGS keep in their handbags. This one ain't lookin' too happy.

It's Romeo say Sis.

What kind of a name is that for a midget dog?

Here, boy. Sis shuffle slowly towards it, holdin' out her finger and thumb like folk do when they approachin' pets. Romeo looks terrified. But he ain't goin' anywhere. He curled up like he bein tryin' to get a sleep, huddled up with his friends in the nice cosy chute.

He belong to Chantelle say Sis. *Girl live on Mustaph's floor.*

Romeo look up at Sis, but he ain't movin' for her. Dog terrified, glued to the spot. She bend and pick him up. Reckon the little beast goin' to nip at her, but he don' do nothin'.

Come on, nothin' more we can do here. Least we can do is get this little fella safely back home. She glance at me. *Get you dressed too. You indecent, boy.*

Muskrat rest a hand on my shoulder. *Sorry you had to fall in there head first, Marsh.* He pauses and adds *Was it a buzz?*

Oh yeah I say. *You oughta try it sometime.*

Hold up say Sis, takin' a couple of pics of the
scene. *Big Auntie goin' to want to see this.*

We headin' up towards our flat, give me chance
to shower and put on some clothes. Feelin' down.
Megabugs been outwittin' us.

*If they been growin' big all summer and now they
ready to take over the block, and they ain't hidin'
down the rubbish chute—*

Then where they been hidin' out? Sis finish the
question for me.

And we still need help. It pretty clear that The
Three Great Detectives ain't exactly of Sherlock
Holmes standard. Compo could do a better job
than us.

On the way up, we pass by His Majesty, skulkin'
roun' the stairwell, lookin' as bad-tempered as ever.
He the only pet in The Finger badassed enough not
to have been taken by the Megas. Ain't sure he even
a pet. Maybe he animal security. He hiss at us, and
flash his claws as we pass by, makin' Sabrebaby
whimper and pull in close to my legs.

We get up to Mus's floor and Sis hand me the
loverdog while she figure which door to knock on,
find Chantelle. Mustaph put his hand forward give ol'
Romeo a pat on the head, and say *Ooh, nice.*

<u>Now</u> what he seen? He reach forward, grab
the pooch's paws, two in each hand, try and prise
them apart like they jammed. Dog got rigor mortis,

ain't even dead.

When I see what attached to Romeo's belly I almos'
drop the dog on the spot.

What the—?

Sabes gives a low snarl, bares his fangs.

What attached to Romeo's belly is three sacks of
blood, look like sausage skin.

As if I hadn't had enough pukiness for one day,
now Romeo gone and got his intestines leakin' all
over my arms.

'Cept these intestines be movin' aroun', like they
alive. They attached to Romeo's belly fur by tiny
snouts. I can see the snouts suckin' away, and the
dog's blood fillin' out the head at the top of each
snout, each head givin' a little jerk, like it swallowin',
and the blood disappearin' into the sack behind it.
Bloodsucker don' even have legs. It jus' a bloodsack
attached by a snoutsucker.

I look at Romeo's eyes, but he ain't lookin' back.
His nights of romance all behind him. Eyes are dead.

Nymphs Sis declares.

Nymphs. Bug eggs. Grown heads so they can start
sucklin' on their own.

<u>Gnarff!</u> Sabre leap up and get his jaws roun'
one of these nymphs, tug it away. He stand there,
chompin' at it, like it sausage fresh from the
butcher's shop. Blood drippin' down from his muzzle.

My dog turnin' cannibal.

I grab one of the remaining nymphs, pull it off

with my hand. It bursts all over, Romeo's blood leakin' down my arm.

Mustaph vomit again, loudly. Thought my pal had stronger stomach than that. I myself find a mos' disgusted groan makin' it way out my lips.

Sis produce her crowbar. *Put the dog on the floor.*

I ain't arguin'.

She whack the last bloodsack with the crowbar, usin' excessive force. Hear a <u>splat</u> and a <u>clang</u> both at the same time. Bloodsack burst, poor dead Romeo covered in his own bloodbath.

Couple of doors open, shocked faces poke out. Horror and disgust.

Mum come around the corner and stop dead in her tracks. I mean <u>dead</u>.

<u>This</u> time, she ain't goin' to deny the evidence in front of her very face.

Doing Time

Romeo! Oh, Romeo! What've you done to my baby!
    Uh-oh.

    Girl with a orange face and freaky long nails come stormin' outta her flat, runnin' her hands through her hair, eyes blazin' like she gonna rip my head off. I know about these type of girl. You do not mess with them. You mos' certainly do not mess with their Chiwowows.

    Mum frozen, open-mouthed, like she ain't quite believin' what her eldest and best gone and done this time.

    Neighbours starin' roun', takin' in the carnage.

    I'm holdin' my hands up, try and placate Orange Girl. Big mistake. Hands covered in Romeo's blood.

    Romeo covered in Romeo's blood.

    My hound got Romeo's blood drippin' from his jaws.

    Mustaph, the idiot, tries – and fails – to stifle a giggle.

    I look to Sis. Sis shrug. Big help.

    What have you done! You animal! Orange Girl lunge for my face, goin' to have my eyes. Sis get a grip on her jus' in time, put her in restraint.

I yell *It's the giant bugs! The giant bugs killed your dog! And their bloodsuckin' babies!*

Orange Girl don't look like she wanna kill me no more. She backin' into Sis's arms. Like she backing away from a <u>highly dangerous individual</u>. In his boxers.

Sabre trots up to me, drops the chewed-up bloodsack, looks up hungrily at me like he beggin' for more. Dumb dog lick his lips.

Sis is forcin' Orange Girl back into her flat, manages to make it look like she <u>assistin'</u> her. Keeps one hand free, take herself a pic of this latest evidence. Out the corner of my eye, I see Mustapha edgin' his way towards the down stairs. Traitor.

That leave me and Mum. She lookin' at the carnage all roun' the floor, and lookin' at me, blood-spattered in my undergarms.

Let me explain I say.

Mum ain't sayin' a word.

But I got plenty to say. *You gotta believe me! This ain't no game. What you think this is – paint? It's blood, Ma, bug blood.*

I'm treadin' a trail of red footsteps all the way to our front door.

Take off your trainers Mum mumbles, stickin' her key in the lock. She pick up the post from the floor.

Is this all she got? Worryin' about dirty footprints?

Listen to me, Ma!

She turns round, totters like she losin' her balance. Her eyes got a sheen, like she about to cry. Muscles workin' in her cheek, chewin' the inside of her face away. *Blood* she whispers.

I'm washin' my hands in the sink. Blood swirlin' away down the plughole. I throw my hands at her, drippin' water. *Clean. See?*

She fixes me with disbelievin' eyes. *What kind of an animal are you?*

She tosses the post down, plonks herself at the table, and the sobs come. *I give up, Marshall, I give up.*

I cross my arms over my chest. What can I say?

I go and shower. Water boilin' hot. Can't seem to soap the stench of animal guts off of me. But it clear my head a little. Once this is all over, I will soak in a bath. Be rid of the filth.

I come back into the kitchen, and Mum say *I give up.*

She already said that. She pressin' her own pause button all the while I was tryin' to defumigate.

We can't give up. I'm lookin' straight at her. *Not now. We bein' attacked. So we fight. Like Dad would have done.*

Stop! Her face streamin'. She got snot bubblin'. *Stop now. Won't you just stop?*

I don' get it. *Mum, we ain't need to be shamed. These bugs don' belong to us. We ain't done it. We ain't dirty. They attackin' the whole block. They killed all the dogs!*

It is like we are not sharin' the same conversation.

Just like him. She smiles, like she cracked some bad-taste joke. *Just like him. I always feared you would be.* She grabs a hold of my wrist, pulls my hand to her face, kisses it. I pull away.

Mum, you got to pull yourself together. We got to think about Connor. Make ourselves safe. Understand?

She laughs, walks over to the balcony doors, looks out. With her back to me, she says *Why do you think Big Auntie went to see the council? Why do you think we've been speaking with the police?*

Mum, this ain't about the little bugs no more. It's about the big bugs. Don't you get it?

Ohh, Marshy... Is like she just ain't hearin' me.

Big bugs. The Megabugs. That killed Sleepy Lady? My son she say, *my eldest son.*

I can't believe she still thinks I'm doin' drugs. What does she think she jus' saw out on the stairs?

Tell me, Mum. Tell me you believe me. Why won't you tell me?

She turn roun', wipin' away her tears. She never used to cry. That one of her things. I seen her carryin' the weight of the world on her back like citizen Atlas, and never cry, not a trickle. Even when the paper called her <u>cheat</u> and the court made her work for no money and she couldn't buy Con-Con new shoes, she never cried.

Oh yeah; 'cept that once, when she caught me teachin' Con-Con how to fight knives.

It's me that makes her cry.

How can I believe you? She look at me straight, through her tears. *You come home covered in blood. Mutilating people's pets, on your own doorstep. How did it get to this?*

She just as shamed as ever. She don't even care I stayed up all night guardin' over Con-Con.

I'm watchin' out for us, Ma. I'll never let any of them things hurt Connor – or you.

No she say, *you are growing up a menace, just like people have been saying. And a danger to those around you.*

She just insultin' me. I look away. I see the mail is addressed for me, so I pick it up and walk into the livin' room, throw myself down on the sofa. Sit there, numb.

I'm done talkin'. I slide my thumb into the flap of my letter, tear it open.

I blink, start again at the beginnin' like I'm in slow class, learnin' ABC. This can't be right. This is a letter from Dad. First letter in ten years. He says he's served his sentence. He's done his time, and they've let him out.

My dad is out of prison. He comin' home. I look up at Mum.

Now we will share the same conversation.

Dad is out of prison. I give her the news.

She surprise me. *I know.*

Mum takes the letter out my hands. She holds her palm out at me when I try and leap up, snatch it back. She readin' it speedy, still with her hand held out to me like lollipop lady stoppin' traffic. Then she look at the envelope, my name and address typed on it nice and neat like she can't believe it. She toss it back at me, like it some scrap.

What do you mean you know? I say.

She don' say nothin'.

He's comin' home, Ma.

She shake her head. *He isn't coming home.*

He is.

He isn't.

Letter lyin' on the floor between us, like a challenge. I got a state of confusion. We been missin' him for ever. Why ain't we leapin' for joy?

What do you mean, Ma? What do you mean, you already know?

Oh Marshall...

She step forward to try and embrace me, but I leap to my feet. *They wrote and told you, didn't they? Yesterday's letter.*

I am slow, tired. Try and compute. *You didn't tell me.* And I picture Mum and Compo, in the doorway last night, so long ago now. *You ... you told Compo.*

I see she still wants to hug me.

YOU TOLD COMPO!

Marshy, you know what he did.

I sit back down. Collapse, like a house of cards. Blown down.

We cope together for a few minutes, with silence. She wants me to say it. She wants to hear it come from my own mouth. She knows we both know it, but we never say the words.

All right, I will.

Yeah I say, fierce. *He killed a man.*

That make her feel any better? Put things right?

He killed a man she whispers back at me.

So I reach out, yeah? I take her hand. *We know that, Mum. But he was jus' defendin' himself, yeah? And now he done his time. This is top, this is the best ever.*

She shakin' her head, over and over, like she can't express enough how much she disagree with me.

Oh, Marshall, please don't be so stupid. How can you refuse to understand?

I'm so through with this. My mum drivin' me insane. I pull my hand back from her.

Look at me, son. Why do you think I never showed you any of his letters?

Letters?

Why do you think we had to move house as soon as the trial was over? Why do you think we never talked about the trial?

From nowhere, tears is wellin' up in my eyes, like I'm soft, like Soft Stuart, like sad boy Ashley whose cheeks I can smash. *You love him!* I bawl.

I loved him she say back. *Marsh, I missed him so*

much, I still miss him, but he's dead, don't you see?
Dead to us. Soon as I found out what he did.

I'm gazin' back at the space where she took down the picture of him that I put up. How come she never liked to talk about him? How come she always hated it when I said I wanted to grow up like him? How come sometime when she looks at me, she has to look away? Why she so shamed of me?

She scratches her arm. She softer now. *I tried so many times to tell you, Marshall. You must have figured it out. Why so many police came for him? Why I hid his letters...*

There she goes with the <u>letters</u> again.

That man that he knifed...

That gangster—

...was his colleague. They were double-crossing.

No! I yell. *It was self-defence. That's why he didn't get a life sentence—*

Marshall, you read it in the newspaper.

You snatched it away from me! It was just a headline. It didn't mean – I couldn't under—

She fix me with a hard-rock stare. *You're going to make me spell it out, aren't you? Even now, you can't admit it to yourself—*

What? What?

Where do you think all the money came from? The dirty money?

What? What?

And the shame. The shame...

Tell me then! You've never told me. Never.
OK then—

I leap up, stomp across the room. Out onto the balcony. I put my hands on the ledge and I pull myself up and I stand, stand tall, like Mus, like Sis, like the rulers of the world. I raise my arms and open my lungs and I scream to God.

I don' want to know. I do not know. None of it is true.

I scream and I scream.

Nothin' comes out. No sound, not a croak. I am a Empty.

Mum is right. I <u>do</u> know. I <u>did</u> guess. I been lyin' all this time. Nothin' I can do to make it any different.

Drugs, isn't it? Always was.

<u>DEALER JAILED.</u> I was too young. <u>FOR KILLING.</u>

He is my dad. I am his son.

Gripped

Time to splatter some Megas. Find where they hidin',
wipe them out. I stomp back into the livin' room. I
snatch up an empty vase – when was the last time
we had flowers, I ask? Smash it against the tabletop.
Shatterin' glass, music to my ears. Mum jus' stand
there, don' try and do nothin'. Dad's letter in her
hand, all crumpled. She don' say a word. She see
my eyes. I'm out the door, lookin' left to right along
the stairways for bugs, shakin' like a bass speaker.
Still got the vase upturned in my hand, jagged and
thirstier than any bug ever be.

Sabre whinin' and growlin', chargin' alongside me.
Come on! COME ON! COME ONNN!

Turn a corner and who do I see out on the
corridor but His Majesty himself.

And two Megabugs.

One of the bugs is crawled out of claw-distance, up
the wall. The other havin' a face off with the hissin',
spittin' puss. Bug tryin' to find space past the cat's
defences, get a thrust in with his nozzle, injec' the
cat so he paralyzed. His Maj lashin' out with his

claws, tryin' to tear the bug's face in two.

Go, cat! Rip those suckers apart!

But the second bug sneak behind His Maj, and ram its nozzle into his flanks. Whole back end go immediately limp. His Maj twist his front end round, lash at the sneaky bug's head. But cat back legs have gone, and he misses. First bug stab him in the neck, and he down.

Cat ain't cool. He start shakin', like he withdrawin' from a full-on Whiskas addiction. His paws hang limp. His tail swish in agitation and his eyes livid. He ain't used to not havin' it all his own way.

Bugs got their two front legs gouged into the cat's fur, schnozzles stabbed in deep like straws in a drinks carton.

I'm hearin' a mos' disgustin' sound. <u>Slurp slurp</u> as them buggies quenchin' a big thirst.

I can't believe they managed to beat His Majesty.

Megabugs concentratin' on their meal, don't notice me. Cat blood fillin' out the bug bodies, swellin' like pumped-up balloons. Skin shiftin' from translucent tan to deep, dark red.

I will kill them.

Cat lookin' up at me. Eyes angry, hopeless. Paws all floopy on account of the bugs paralyzed him with their venom. Narked. Sucked out. Robbed. Tip of his tail swishin' like crazy. Starin' wide-eyed in indignity.

I will kill them.

Life fades out of the eyes. Spark gone. Somethin'

switched off inside his head. Ain't His Majesty no more, just another Empty.

First Megabug braces its knee joints, pullin' its snout out of the cat. <u>Squelch.</u> One drip of blood hangin' off the end of the schnozzle. Bug gives a short snort, sucks it up.

Second bug follows suit. They fix their red-eyed gaze on me.

I will smash them.

Bugs start to turn, escape.

Creeps ain't so fast as the suckers on Sis's balcony. Carryin' a fresh bellyful, can only waddle like two-ton fatboys exitin' McDonalds.

Shattered base of the vase feelin' good in my hand.

His Maj is lyin' there all flat. Lookin' like a fluffy scarf for a posh lady's neck.

I cut one bug off from the other side of the dead cat. Bug is trapped, nowhere to go.

Stab its head. Smash it like a mega crème egg. Head yolk slip out over its devil eyes.

Other bug ain't goin' far. I lift up my foot, slam my trainer down on the bug's back. <u>Clunk.</u> Bug bend its knees under the pressure, give me the evils, wagglin' its antennas. Now I made it <u>really</u> angry. I flinch at the look that Megabug throw me. That bug exoskeleton immune even to the stomp of good quality Nike. How nasty is that?

Not as nasty as me. Not as angry as me.

I kick it.

I kick it in the eye, and I kick it in the belly. Kick its shell. Its head.

Exoskeleton tough enough, but when it shatter, it shatter like a popped lightbulb.

Second-hand cat juice spurt up my legs. Fragment of shell clitter-clatter across the floor. Blood spread in a puddle aroun' me. Belly fumes fill my nostrils. Gassin' me. Around its popped bodysack its legs wigglin', shakin' what left of its busted head, wantin' to scuttle away, flee from death.

So?

I kick it some more. Kick it with my left foot, kick it with my right. I kick it, one two, one two. Keep on kickin'. Kickin' so it no more than litter on the floor, stain on the wall. Kick at the wall. Kick everythin'.

Nex' thing I know, I'm on the ground, a weight on my back, pushin' my face into the floor. My weapon gone flyin' out my hand, rolled where it can't do me no good.

Hot breath in my ear.

Wiggle and thrash but no matter what, I can't shake the weight. They can suck me and drain me now, I don' care, but let me kill some more of them first. I roar. I can kill another, just one, with my hand, rip its head. My howlin' echoin' down the hallway like a ghost.

Easy, boy. Easy.

Sis.

Easy. Easy.

Can't make myself stop strugglin', even though I know it Sis on my back. She slip her hands under my armpits, up and roun' the back of my neck, linkin' her fingers into a Half-Nelson, all the time whisperin' warm whispers into my head.

My head in a puddle, soakin' my cheeks and my hair. Not blood though. I'm cryin' now, ain't I? Sobbin' like a infant.

You heard, then? Sis's words gentle in my ears. She knows about my dad. Sis always know everythin' before anyone else, same as Big Auntie.

Same as Compo.

Everybody know about my dad but me!

She strokin' my hair and her grip relax into a hug.

She lie there with me in the stairway, holdin' me firm.

Sis sit on me for half an hour, waitin' until I get bored of bein' enraged. Every five minute she loosen her grip and I'm <u>sure</u> I can throw her off, set myself free. Every time, I am mistaken.

You will thank me for this say Sis.

Sure I say. *One day I'll return the favour, sit on you all afternoon when you got business to do.*

I feel her breath warm on my neck. Think of my mum.

Why does everybody lie? I ask Sis.

I'm tellin' the truth she say, tightenin' the grip on her Half-Nelson.

Why did my mum tell you about Dad, but not me?

She didn't. She telled Big Auntie. Big Auntie telled me because she tell me everythin'. I ain't no use otherwise.

Why my mum tell Compo?

Silence. She thinkin' about this one.

Maybe she say, *she thought Compo could help.*

Oh, OK. And I make my move, manage to get a grip of her head, heave my body up and to the right, break her grip, roll on top. Before she know it, I got my knees on her shoulders, pinnin' her down.

She know she been out-manoeuvred. Don' waste energy resistin'.

Compo ain't no friend. How she trustin' him before she trustin' me?

Sis playin' possum. Catch me off guard. Jerk her whole body upwards, try and buck me off. I smile. I am wise. Hold steady. She surrender again. *Well?*

Marsh she say, gaspin' for her breath back, *trust is somethin' you earn. Your ma trusts Compo because he is the biggest pain in the ass in The Finger. He earned his trust. He dreams of bein' boss of Scotland Yard.*

He is a fat fool!

True. And Muskrat is a skinny fool. Bein' a fool don' mean you can't be trustworthy. It jus' mean you come up with dumb-ass ideas. You learn that today.

I been learnin' too much.

Maybe. Answer me this. Do you think your mum trusted your dad?

Course she did!

She says no more. Lets that one sit with me a bit.

Mum <u>should</u> trust me. I take care of her. And Connor. I fight for her. I watch her. Mum knows she can trust me. She can.

I'm gettin' pins and needles say Sis.

I am <u>not</u> a fool. We need a plan.

How about we go in, make a cup of tea? say Sis, breathless and bored.

I climb off her, offer my hand to help her up. She takes it.

She twists my arm up behind my back, so it shrieks with pain. Double-cross. *Say <u>Sis wins</u>* she laughs in my ear. *Say <u>Sis wins</u>.*

Sis wins! Sis wins!

Damn. Shoulda seen that comin'.

Let's get that tea she says, makin' the <u>loser</u> sign at me with her finger and thumb.

In Sis's room, back in her flat, she ain't talkin' no more about Dad – what more is there for her to say? Sis know that everybody got a expert opinion about my dad. Only he himself is expert on the subject. When we beat the bugs, I will find my dad. I will listen to genuine expert opinion, because I am not to be taken as a fool.

When we beat the bugs.

We sittin' on the edge of Sis's bed, drinkin' tea, starin' at her bedroom rug. She cuppin' her mug in both hands, her eyes fix on me like she still got me in the firmness of her grip, ain't lettin' me go.

Sabre sittin' close as he can, his thick neck leanin' into my thigh. He stock-still also, like he thinkin' about best plan of action, chewin' it over like a bone.

Sis showin' me all the footage she taken. The dead pets overflowin' out the rubbish chute, the popped bloodsacks of the nymphs, and – caught on camera – me kickin' the daylight outta the two Megas that killed the cat.

Not much left of them, after you stomped 'em. You certainly got a habit of screwin' aroun' with our evidence, don't you, boy?

I take that as praise. *You show Big Auntie?*

No. She still out on her missions. Ain't takin' no calls.

Why she gone off now of all times? We need her.

She know what she doin'. Meanwhile, I put these beauties on my phone, been sendin' it to everybody I know in The Finger. A call for action. Posted it on Facebook too.

So word is out? We got believers.

Sis grimace. *If someone sent you images like this, what'd you think?*

I'd think I got better things to worry about than lookin' at some nonsense some fool put together on Photoshop. It look like one of Mustaph's models.

'Zackly. But Big Auntie gettin' all these updates. She be figurin' things.

Unless Big Auntie come on board, we is deeply in the proverbials. We got zero credibility. I ain't assisted matters by turnin' stomp-crazy in my undergarms. Least I was dressed again by the time Sis filmed me batterin' the Megas.

Anybody start takin' this serious I say, *I'll eat my dog.*

Sabre whines, like he heard me. I pat his head.

Sis say *Only hope we got is that the Megas are puttin' in more of an appearance. They gettin' careless – or cocky – and sightin's on the increase. Megas just a rumour, but rumour spreadin' rapid.*

She give me a deep look, check I'm focusing and not losin' it. Believe me, I am focused. I am focusin' on the problem the way my dad would have focused. Back in the day. I got to be like I imagine he would be.

Got to imagine.

Marsh? She click her fingers. *We got to get people workin' in groups, we got to be armed, organized, but people only goin' to act on Big Auntie's word, and Big Auntie away missionin'.*

I'm only half listenin'. Dad's letter didn't say whether or not he was goin' to come over to The Finger. Just said that he was out of prison, wanted to say hi.

Them that have <u>seen</u> the Megas, doin' their best to put the word out, tell people keep their windows closed. Better still, vacate the premises. Best place for *people now is far away from The Finger they can get.*

What if Dad choose to come get me, take me away from Mum and Con-Con and Sabre? Become <u>bad bwoi</u> with him and his crew?

You listenin' to me? Sis sayin'.

Sure. My mouth is movin'. Say words Sis wantin' to hear. *We goin' to defend the block.*

She peerin' at me close, scrutinization. *Mallow? You need a lie-down?*

She's right. I ain't had no sleeps, have I? Been up since yesterday. No matter, our homes is bein' invaded and we got responsibilities. Ain't no Mega goin' to do to my family what I see them do to His Majesty.

Don' worry 'bout me I say. *I'm ready for battle.*

Oh she say. *Actually I would like you to very slowly turn your head to your left. Don' say a word, jus' look, no sudden movement.*

Uh-oh.

I turn my head. Look across her floor.

Higher.

Look to her bedroom window. See clear blue sky framed by gloss paint. Two straight bits of wire stickin' down, like TV aerial. Thicker rod between 'em. Right by the edge, jus' visible, two red globes, cherries.

Room is bugged say Sis.

At the bottom of the window, the same, only TV aerials stickin' up 'stead of down. Same bright cherries.

Two of the suckers.

Sis move her hand slowly up from under the bed. Baseball bat. 'Mazin' how many of us in The Finger keep wooden bats under our beds, even though no one I know actually play baseball.

I give the count of three she whisper. *You fling the window open, duck straight down.*

I'm with her.

Three!

We move like pros. Two seconds, Sis swingin' her bat directly where the bottom bug's bodysack waitin' for a poppin'.

Damn. She bring her arm back in, disappointed.

I stick my head out the window. We look up, down, and lef' to right. Not a bug in sight. Fast as lightnin'.

Down on the ground, we see a council works van pullin' up.

Hey, lookee here say Sis. *Don' see one of them very often. Maybe Big Auntie persuaded the council send someone check out what we all been claimin'.*

Maybe. I ain't convinced. More likely they jus' come evict someone who behind with the rent.

Let's go see. You up for that, Marsh?

I'm sweet, Sis. Come on, let's call on Mustaph on the way down, see if he can keep me awake with his repartee and wit.

So me and Sis and my dog headin' down to the ground floor. Down and round we goin', down and round. Mos' days, stairwell don't cause me no bother. Today I got me a dizzy feelin' in my head, feel like

I'm gonna stumble, gonna fly, float. Like my head
under invasion as well as The Finger.

Wait in the stairwell, while Sis drag out Muskrat,
grumblin' – she disturbed his meditations. Voices
fuzzy in my ears, like I ain't shaken out all of them
bugs from the rubbish chute.

Down and roun', down and roun'. Bug bullet
holes in the walls aroun' us. Ain't nothin' else but
the helter-skelterin' of our footsteps, Sabretooth's
unclipped claws, clickety-clackin' roun' the stairwell,
like we an army of hundreds, ready to do battlin' with
the invaders. Who goin' to try snatch our territory off
of us?

From behind a MISSING DOG poster pinned to a
wall, a Megabug suddenly bolt out, waggle its feelers
at us, and make a run for it, like it jus' toyin' with us.

Down on the ground floor we see two clowns in
boilersuits. They from the council, carryin' a big
toolbox full of crowbars, screwdrivers and spanners.

Yo say Muskrat.

Yo answer one of the boilersuits sarcastically.
We're here for the lift?

Meat men finally got tired of strugglin' with them
bodies up and down the stairs. Persuaded the council
come and do somethin' about it.

Step this way say Sis, and waves them in.

The Gates of Hell

Don't look like these jokers know how to fix a light
bulb in a light fittin', nor step on no stool to do it,
never mind no tower-block lift that ain't even lifted
a finger in months. Still, we lean back against the
concrete pillar, fold our arms and watch 'em.

Boilersuit Number One, sportin' a 'ceedingly
helpful nametag ANDY, frown at us like he thinkin'
What, are we a circus act now, entertainment for
the youth?

Boilersuit Number Two, nametagged RACHID, says
Last job of the day, had to be the lousiest. He throws
us a filthy look, like we responsible for bustin' our
own lift. He open up his box of tricks, bring out two
crowbars and what look like a mega drill. Instead
of a point, this tool got extendible metal grips, all
snuggled tight like – well, bugs in a rug.

Sis got a look of great interest on her face as Andy
and Rachid huffle and puffle and sweat and grunt,
each tryin' to wedge his crowbar into the middle of
the lift doors, get themselves a good grip, persuade
them doors to part. Rachid manages to thrust his

magical metal wedge into the incey gap between the doors, with a satisfactory smirk. He begins pumpin' the handles like Edward Scissorhands cuttin' down a hedge. As he does, the gap in the lift doors gettin' wider and wider. Andy is leanin' in, gettin' all Vin Diesel and *Uurgh*in' them doors further open with bare hands.

Suddenly, the doors open fully, 'zackly as they should. Andy and Rachid fall back, as a foulness billows out. They drop their tools, turn and tumble towards us. The foulness overtakes them, reaches us leanin' comfy 'gainst our pillar. The stink is like the bins behind the butcher's shop, if you had your head stuffed in 'em, face first. Bug smell.

Andy pulls himself together first, feeds us a look of disgust. *You bloody animals. You don' deserve housin'. You should be locked in a zoo.*

What? He think this is the smell of the citizens of The Finger havin' done their business in the lift for six months? Man out of his mind.

Rachid got himself more together than his workmate. *Always the same* he mutters, reachin' into his toolbag, pullin' out disposable breathin' mask, and plastic gloves, like they are used to findin' people's doin's when they fixin' up lifts.

Hey, Rachid say Sis.

He stop, turn to look at her.

You don' wanna go back there.

She right say Mus. *Bad business.*

Is that so? Andy cuts in. *Why don't you kids do us a favour, go off and loot Argos or something, yeah?*

Listen say Sis, and listen good. *We got a big nest of giant bugs somewhere in the building, and smells to me like you might of found it.* She puttin' on her most authoritative voice, doin' her best to be convincin'. They got any brains, they be convinced. *Why don' one of you fellas get on your radio and call back-up, yeah?*

Do one says Andy. Rachid jus' grunts, walks towards the lift shaft.

No Sis shakin' her head. *You do not want to do that.*

You youth tryin' to give us orders? asks Andy. *Why exactly shouldn't we want to look in the lift shaft?*

The bugs will eat you alive.

Andy sneers. This level of disbelief been our problem from the minute the bugs first appeared. You a youth, adults jus' won' believe you. You a youth from The Finger, you lyin' with malice.

I repeat Sis's words. *The bugs will eat you alive.*

Andy shoots razor-blade glare at me, like he thinks I'm <u>darin'</u> him.

Watch me he says, walks forward. Rachid steps forward with him.

Rachid Sis say, *they goin' to eat you alive.*

But he don' even turn around. They walk slowly forward towards the lip of the lift shaft. Peer in. I admit, I'm grimacin'. They lean in and look down. Now I know what is meant in books when they go on about <u>my heart was in my mouth</u>.

They squintin' in, adjustin' their eyes to the dark. I'm waitin' for the worst. Andy says *Oh, Jesus. Christ.*

What is it? says Rachid.

It's...

Sis catches my eye. She's ready for everythin'. Got her mobile primed.

...absolutely disgusting. He take a big step back.

A nymph, not much past egg stage, crawlin' out of the shadows. 'Bout four inches long, mostly consistin' of bloodsack. Little legs ain't yet fully formed. Sorta <u>wigglin</u>' more than crawlin'.

Rachid strides forward. *Filth!* He stamps his boot down on the nymph, and it disintegrates with a bloody squelch. *This whole place is sick* he say. *You need fumigators. The lot of you.*

I hear a rumble from overhead. Step back. Rumble gettin' louder. Take two steps back. Andy and Rachid peer upwards into the shaft. Sis starts filming. I run back.

A big shadow tumbles down from the lift shaft, coverin' the council men in gloom.

The shadow is bugs. The shadow is a mass of starvin' Megas, pourin' down the lift shaft like baked beans from a tin. Andy and Rachid don't even get to cuss, jus' gasp in 'mazement as a ton of Megas fall onto their shoulders, pile around their feet, beginnin' to climb and bite.

This is where they been hidin' all this time, cosyin'

up in the lift shaft. Bidin'.

Never seen so many bugs. They are a army. They keep droppin', wave after wave, from the shaft of the lift. A invadin' force.

Andy straight away tumble like a slap-sticked clown, pulled in towards the lift. Swallowed.

Rachid drop to his knees. A bug is crawlin' over his face, its underbelly mufflin' his scream. It gouges its claws into his ears, its own face hoverin' for a second, focusing on his eyes, before plungin' its proboscis right through, deep into his brain. It sucks.

Sis stops filming.

The mass come swarmin' towards us, crawlin' along the walls, sweepin' across the floor, unstoppable as a tsunami tide.

Ruuuun! yells Sis.

Sabretooth is way ahead of us.

Self-Defence Technique Number Four

We run.

Past the council van, left with its light blinkin' like it in a perpetual state of confusion.

Past the smashed-up fence surroundin' the smashed-up swings and slides.

Past the rundown corner shop with its emptied tubs of choc chip.

Past the scrubby hedge decorated with dog-poo bags. The hedge is officially the end of Finger territory.

We run towards the local school before Sis look back behind her, and grab a hold of my shoulder. *Wait up.*

We stop. Puff and pant and sweat. Eyes dartin' all around us. Hackles up.

Whole view eerily quiet. No sign of any Megabugs. Just empty kebab cartons clatterin' along like tumbleweed. Late-day sun dippin' down behind distant estates. Gloom descendin'.

Can't help it, keep lookin' down at my feet, sure those beasties be crawlin' their way up my ankles.

Mus jabberin' and shiverin' like a boy possessed.
Stop it, you two Sis order us. *You gettin' me at it too.*

Fair point. There ain't no Megas to be seen. Not a single one come <u>pitter-pattin'</u> after us. Like they not ready yet to show themselves outside the block.

We catch our breath.

What we done is: we run away.

I am <u>yellow</u>.

Sis starin' at me with a fierce look on her face. I swear sometimes we can read each other's brains. Sis ain't no coward, no more than me. Our families are over there, in The Finger, with the bugs.

'Stead of comin' chasin' out after us, they gone up. Up towards our homes. Our people.

Come she say.

We start runnin' back, all the while keepin' our eyes out, scannin' the territory for the enemy. When we get near to the blinkin' council van, Sis grab my arm, stop me. She gimme a wink.

Before I can stop her, she climbs in. Mus leaps in after her. I'm keepin' lookout, listenin' to them rummagin' round inside. *Mostly porno mags and beer bottles in here, Marsh* say Mus.

Sis say *Here we are. Catch!*

Sis type of girl who throw things at you without checkin' first that you ready to do some catchin'. I'm used to it, throwin' my arms up front just in time to receive a Thor-sized claw hammer. I weigh it up in my hands. This could smash a lot of Megas. Safe. Sis climb back out, herself clutchin' what looks like the baddest-assed nail gun.

Mustaph clamber after her wearin' a hard hat and wieldin' a ... Fast Foam Big One?

Sis fire a practice shot of her nail gun without warnin', damn near give me a ear piercin' that I ain't paid for. Nail appear dead centre of a council notice board, ten feet behind me: NO BALL GAMES. NO CYCLING. NO SKATEBOARDING. NO BARBECUES et cet. Don't say nothin' about no nail guns.

Mustaph squirt his Fast Foam Big One gun at the nail. Foam squirt over it, instantly expandin' and hardenin'. He grins.

Sis tuck whole box full of nails inside her hoodie. Gesturin' back at The Finger, she gimme that look.

Mus throwin' Steven Seagal poses with his Foam Gun.

Sis grins at me. *Dare ya?*

Oh yeah, I'm darin'.

We ain't runnin' out on our people, see? Them bugs want a turf war, they goin' to get a turf war.

I ain't gonna let these suckers get anywhere near Mum and Connor.

I'm a hundred per cent pysched, anticipatin' diggin' the claw end of this hammer into a Mega shell, like a old-school oil prospector. <u>Sploosh.</u>

My head itchin', itchin' like I been bit all inside my ears, across the top, round behind my eyes. Scratch it. Scratch it. I got littl'uns tryin' to escape through my nose, feet ticklin' me. I push a finger up, squish it against my nostril.

Listen up. They crawled in my ears. Listen now. <u>Scritch-scritch.</u> Chewin' and clawin' through my earwax, burrowin' in, <u>scritchin'</u> towards my brains.

They got inside. They invaded. <u>Scritch scritch.</u> Through our windows and between our sheets and and behind the sink, bitin' and suckin' and pooin' scattershot bullet holes. <u>Blam.</u> <u>Blam.</u> In my head.

We are bug fodder. Junk.

Marsh?

Sis is pullin' my arms offa my head. I'm scratchin'—

Marsh!

We never goin' to be rid. So we fight...

Marshall! She squeezin' my wrists.

...to the death.

She pick up the mallet I dropped and she place it back in my hands.

Swing it she say. *Feel.*

I ain't gonna itch and scratch. I'm gonna <u>swing</u> and <u>smash</u> and <u>shatter</u> and <u>splat</u>.

Self-Defence Technique Number Four: Total Onslaught.

We swing open the doors and charge in, tools raised, war cries whoopin'.

There ain't zero to see. No Megas. No Andy. No Rachid. Lift doors still wide open, black hole within. Who gonna take a peek inside?

Mus? I say.

Uh-unh. No way.

We all go together say Sis. *Have our weapons set. Be ready to strike the second you seen one of 'em. If one of us strikes, we all strike, get me?*

We getcha.

Step by step, inch by inch. Silence is eerie. Closer. Closer.

Only thing repellin' us is the stench. I'm wishin' we'd grabbed some masks while we was busy toolin' ourselves up. Too late now. Tryin' not to breath – tricky, when your heart beatin' 140 bpm.

Lift is empty.

There ain't nothin' to hear. No ominous rumblin' nor creepy <u>pitter-pats</u>.

They gone.

Whooh. Mustaph breathe out, long and deep.

See what else gone too? I say. *Our friends Andy and Rachid. Sly Megas gone and hidden their bodies somewhere, so as not to raise the alarm.*

<u>*We*</u> *the ones goin' to raise the alarm* say Sis.

A lone Megabug dashes out from behind a pillar, makin' a break for it. Must have been lef' behind by its mates. Maybe it lef' behind as a spy.

<u>SPLOTT!</u>

Swear I never seen Muskrat move so fast. He like a highly trained assassin. Blob of foam spit straight out the end of his foam gun, hit that Mega directly on its back. Whole thing blow up like a air bag in a car.

Nex' second, there ain't no bug to see, just one foamy mess. Look like a accident at a bubblegum factory.

He ain't got nothin' to report say Mus, blowin' imaginary smoke away from the barrel of his gun.

We movin' around in small circles, checkin' all the space around us. It too quiet.

They gonna pounce?

Sis hold her hand up for total silence. We listen and we watch. Where they gone? I got my hammer raised, ready for 'em.

Woof! say Sabe. I know for certain the area is now free of Megas. Sabe only ever barks at enemies once they gone away.

They gone up. Up into The Finger. Into position.

It beginning to get dark I say.

Makin' their battle formations.

We runnin' out of time.

We race up the stairwell, keepin' eyes peeled and weapons raised. Don' see no giant bugs. See plenty of bullet-hole poo. They <u>been</u> here. Maybe they makin' their way to the outside walls, wait outside all the open windows, pounce as one when darkness falls.

We reach the seventh floor, still no sign of where they hidin' out. Mus say *I'm goin' to try and persuade my folks to leave. Figure somewhere for 'em to go.*

Sis say *Wait up.* She bring out her phone. *I send you the film of the lift men, so your family more easy to persuade.*

Ain't got no phone, have I? shrug Mus.

How many times I told you you need a phone?
I tusk.

He shrug again.

Sis I say, *you gonna send that film to your whole address book? Ain't no one gonna doubt us now.*

She press a button. *Is done.*

Now we in business. I put a hand on Mustaph's shoulder. *Good luck, yeah? And thanks, Mus. Maybe we'll meet up tomorrow, when everyone safe.*

What you talkin' about? He give me his affronted look. *I ain't goin' nowhere. Get my folks out is all. You think I'm goin' to bail on you now? We got work to do.*

Thought you hated work, Musky? Sis say.

Certainly. But – he blow a big raspberry – *sometimes there just ain't no dodgin' it. Meet you in Sis's place, yeah?*

That my boy.

We all slippin' skin. Bugs ain't goin' to beat us. Ain't got no chance.

Come say Sis, and me, her and the dog run on up.

It is time to bring Mum on side.

Laughing Stock
of the Cop Shop

She ain't in.

Where is she? She always in. Con-Con ain't here either. Where are they? Me and Sis search the flat from top to bottom, Sabre sniffin' for 'em also.

I phone her. Her phone rings on the kitchen table. Why ain't she taken it with her, wherever she gone?

I don' like it, Sis. I don' like it at all.

Sis try and sound all reassurin'. *She probably jus' down the corner shop, is all, taken your bro with her so she know he safe.*

She plonk herself down on the sofa. *Let's jus' sit and wait a while. I'll see if I can get through to Big Auntie, yeah? Make sure she got the video.*

But before Sis gets chance to call Big Auntie, there's a hammerin' at the door. I almos' leap out of my skin.

I pick up the hammer and I'm ready to use it.

I pull open the door.

Wish I had a thinkin' brain as well as a battlin' one. Before I even realize my name ain't Clever Trevor, my hammer is lyin' on the floor and I got hands on my collar shovin' me up agains' the door.

Compo. He was expectin' me.

Maybe he was too quick for me, but I should have anticipated it, yeah? Gonna end up gettin' my blood slurped by Megas if I don't sharpen myself up, leave Con-Con as a only child. Punch my own head if I had a hand free.

Found you he say. He got the bug schnozzle in his hand from before, and wavin' it furiously in front of my face, like I am the fool and not him. *You let me make a right berk of myself, didn't you!* he yells.

Easy, Officer Cotton. Sis raise her nail gun, and set Compo in her sights. *Nice and easy, you don' want to see me display my DIY skills, do you now?*

I do. I could happily picture old Compo gettin' nailed to the wall, like a certificate of top neighbourliness.

Easy girl echo Compo, nice and careful, like he an expert on this type of negotiable situation.

No Sis insist. *You take it easy. We got two more men been taken by the giant bugs, and now they lyin' in wait for the rest of us. That's why we armed. That's why we on the same side as you. Get me? You want the video evidence?*

No need says Compo. *That's why I've been seeking you out.*

What you mean? say Sis.

Put down the gun and I'll tell you.

Put down my friend and I'll put down my gun.

Compo show he a man of perfec' manners. He even straighten my shirt for me. Then he wave the bug schnozzle in front of our noses. *You two know how much humiliation you've caused me with this?*

I laugh. *Told you it wasn't no drug pipe.*

So I was told, <u>after</u> I handed it over to the drug squad. Imagine that?

Me and Sis can't help but share a giggle. Boy, is Compo in a fluster. He stamp his feet, he so agitated.

All right, all right, it's not that funny. I'm trying to do my duty here! That's why I decided to examine it more closely.

I can see he actually tryin' not to blush. Never seen Compo so embarrassed. After a mo', he fix his gaze on Sis, try and give her his mos' mature, responsible look. It killin' me tryin' not to laugh. *Young lady* he say. *Sensible now. Please. Is this ... is this or is this not a ... proboscis?*

Pow. How long has it taken for us to get someone to finally believe what goin' down? At last, a adult ready to accep' the truth. Me and Sis are struck-dumb.

Compo take that silence as a encouragin' sign. He go on. *Because, when I gave this opinion in my report, the Commander, well, he ... he...*

It too much for me. I burst into uncontrollables. Man, I am creasin' up. Sis starts up too. We are in hysterics. Floodin' tears. Oh my daze.

Compo. What a tool. Finally he see sense and what do he do? He present himself as the laughin' stock of the Cop Shop. He is livid at our laughin' but we cannot stop.

A giant bug drops from the ceilin' onto his head. Two front legs gouge into his cheeks, the proboscis tappin' against his nose and his mouth tryin' to find a angle to stab him, paralyze his head.

Whoah. My hammer is lyin' on the floor.

Keep still say Sis.

Comp is doin' the Death Fandango. She raises her gun and shoots a nail right between the Mega's eyes, sendin' it flyin' against the door, where it hangs, pinned like a exhibit in a bug display.

Sabretooth throws me one look of absolute terror. It is his last straw, broke the mongrel's back. He flip, bolt through the door, up the stairs, fast as he can.

Sabe! I give Compo one last look. *You call the _real_ police, yeah? And you wait here for my mum. Tell her what really goin' down. You owe me!* And I race after my dog.

I should consider the consequence of racin' off after Sabre. I am so tired. I do not consider the consequence.

Top of the Beanstalk

Far as I'm concerned, 'part from Mum and Con, I got
three more family, that Sis, Mus and Sabretooth. We
is one and all, and I ain't leavin' my dog panicked
and alone at the mercy of the Megas. He ain't goin'
to survive two minutes. I got in my mind what they
done to His Maj. Picturin' the same with Sabes break
my heart.

We got to impose a conclusion to this madness.
Finger is our territory, no way we lettin' some six-leg,
red-eye crew take it over. We have final showdown:
friends, family against bloodsuckers.

All we got to do is find where they gone. My mind
is pushin' me. Where are the bugs? If they ain't hidin'
no more in the lift shaft? Think I know. They hidin'
everywhere now. Squeezin' through windows, hidin'
'neath folks' mattresses, on top of their cupboards,
snuggled in the air space between DVD players,
Xbox games, sittin' sneaky in pots and pans beneath
the sink, waitin' to creep out, attach themselves to
unsuspecting legs.

Boundin' up, my mind pushin' me, givin' me grief

like I surely deserve. <u>I shoulda done this. I shoulda done that.</u> Whole world gone apocalyptic from the moment I smashed Ashley in his brain-damaged mouth.

Sabe! I call. *Sabe! Heel, boy!*

Stupid dog. Up we race, eleventh, twelfth, past the thirteenth floor, a Empty's flat cordoned off with police tape. Higher, past a panickin' family on the fourteenth, brothers, sisters, mum and dad, all of 'em carryin' bags and cases and lookin' dazed. They scurry past, like frightened rats. Word got out at last.

Go easy! I yell. *Get as far as you can, yeah?*

One of the boys raise his eyebrows at me in response. Boy I know from school. *I'll text you* I add, like a fool. Old habits.

I speed up the next flight.

<u>Puff puff puff</u> I'm goin', exhaustion catchin' up with me, puttin' weights on my legs and a clamp on my chest. <u>Puff puff</u> like I smoke cigarettes 40 a day. Ears are wacko, playin' havoc with my balance. Higher I go, higher, nowhere to go but up in the world. Bug bullet holes blurrin' past my head, dirty suckers turnin' whole block into a public toilet.

Sabretooth! Here, boy! Heel! What Sabe goin' to do when he get to the top, keep on boundin' up into the clouds? Dogs never think things through.

Seventeenth floor, big man on his knees with a axe, choppin' up a pile of Megas. Mad Gaz, wearin' only a vest and one sock, choppin' away like he plannin' on putting all them Megas in a pie, swivel-eyed and sweaty.

Nice one, bro.

Higher. And round. Higher. And round.

Goin' against the tide of more and more families packin' their bags and hurryin' down. Sis's video makin' its impression felt.

Hearin' my breath wheezing like I is enjoyin' full-blown cardiac here on the steps, usin' cuss words my mum banned from earshot.

Sabretooth! I yell.

I am thirteen miles high. I am leavin' everythin' behin', what was my world, goin' where I don' know.

I trip, dodgin' some fool's wheelie case.

My messed-up head whack my balance. Don't put my hands out in time to break my fall. Nose is coshed full-on by the edge of the stair. <u>BAM!</u>

Damn if I ain't now experiencin' what they mean in books when they say <u>you seein' stars</u>. My up seem to be down, and my in seem to be out. Ohhh...

Pair of hands reachin' round beneath my ribs and my pits, and I'm floatin' up. Hands be like juggler's hands, spinnin' me round like I'm as light as a Empty mus' be. Hands carryin' me further up, not down where everyone fleein'. I don' get it, 'cos as I turn in the air I see my old photograph of Dad that I keep beneath the mattress.

But it ain't the same. Face is thinner, hair is greyer. Eyes ain't got that mischievous spark.

<u>Whump.</u> My belly landin' against the muscle of those same broad shoulders. His fingers on the small of my back, keepin' me balanced. My eyes fuzzying a picture of his back and legs as we jig-jig up and up the final flights. I'm hearin' his voice. *Hello, boy. Hold on tight, 'cos we goin' right to the top.*

After all these years, here I am, back on my dad's shoulders. Only it ain't how I remember it, nor how I imagined it. I ain't King of the Castle no more. Blood rushin' down to my head. All I'm seein' is the end of everythin'. All I'm smellin' is a sickness, runnin' right through the block, my friends, my family and me.

Up we go. My giant dad takin' me up the top of the beanstalk.

Intravenous

Dad don't smell the same way as I remember. He
smell like rank sweat and stale tobacco. Fumin' from
his jacket and his pits, it is nauseous. My dad used to
smell like summer mornin'. This is true, I swear.

He ain't carryin' me straight. When I was little
it was like we won the World Cup and I was <u>raised</u>
on his shoulder, like a proper champ. Right now, he
lurchin' and uneven. Side of my head keep bangin'
against his back, which is feelin' all knobbled,
like somethin' twisted his bones and they ain't
set straight. My busted nose throbbin' against his
roughness.

Family pet runnin' excitedly by our side, like a
advert for supermarkets.

Luckily, he ain't got far to take me. How Dad know
about the Attic Office, I don't know. Maybe he got the
same enquirin' mind as me and my crew. But here
we are, Dad pushin' open the door and smell of old
pee waftin' out at us.

Yap, yap! go the doggie. We be the picture of bliss.

Dad shrug me off his shoulder onto a dirty old

mattress. I'm thinkin' this the safest place to be, ain't no Megabug goin' to be insane enough to hidey-hole in this stinky beddin'.

Got to get my head straight. Defuzzify myself.

Dad wedges the door shut behind us. Only my family got brains enough to spot the door behind the corner of the top flat. Just us havin' fun playin' hide-n-seek among the smashed-up furniture, away from the illness of the world.

Dad slump down onto the office chair. I can see he's knackered. Two flights he carried me up, and he's done. He give me the appraisals. Look like a school teacher, retired due to ill-health. Plonked behind the desk, like he about to teach me a lesson I'll never forget.

I'm givin' him appraisals also.

He ain't as gigantic as I remember, nor nowhere near as strong. He doesn't have my dad's eyes. He got somebody else's eyes.

He says *You've changed.*

You too.

He give a twisted smile. *Couldn't believe it when I hear your voice, callin' out. Bugs after you too?*

Sabes is whinin', locked out behind the wedged shut door.

That my dog I say.

Dad curls his lip. *He snapped at me.* He pauses. *I hate dogs.*

Sabre is my pet.

194

Dad don't answer. We listen to Sabre scratchin' to be let in. I try and stand, go to the door.

Leave it.

I'm exhausted. He safe enough for a minute. *How long you been out? Of prison.*

He focuses on the wall behind me. *Long enough to get myself sorted.* He perk himself up for a moment. *Hey, look like I arrive in the nick of time. Come here.*

He fishin' aroun' in his pockets and after a moment he bring out a tissue. It is stained. He wipes the blood off my nose. He holds my chin with the tips of his fingers. Inspectin'. He has dirt grimed in his nails. Open my mouth to invite him down to shower, freshen up, and he say:

How's your mother?

His eyes got a gleam. I can't tell if he's lookin' mean or hopeful. I 'member one afternoon, long time ago, sittin' with Sis and she was tryin' to explain to me the meanin' of the word <u>bitter</u>. I couldn't grasp it. Now I'm sittin' wonderin' if the look in my dad's eye is a <u>bitter</u> look. Corner of his mouth wobble slightly, and I'm sorry for him.

She got the hump with you I say.

He don't say nothin'.

It is stressful times right now I say.

Tell me about it.

We got infestation I say.

He shake his head. I am the fool. When he say <u>tell me about it</u> he mean <u>you think you got it tough</u>. He don't mean me to tell him about it.

So? he say. *Bugs get bigger every day. These're worse than I ever seen, but don't you worry. We're safe up here. And I got all I need. All we need.*

What's he talkin' about?

I got a brother I say.

He don't say nothin' to that.

He's called Connor.

He rolls his eyes. *Named after his mother.*

I'm wonderin' if he goin' to help us. We got a emergency situation down the stairs. Dad fishes around in his pockets. *I'm achin'* he say. *Too much bug-dodgin'. Bad business.* He brings out a stick of chewin' gum. Looks at me weird and say *Want some?*

I shake my head. I wanna know where he been, what he been up to. What are we goin' to do now that he's back? We goin' to fight those Megas side by side?

I ask him *How was it?* and he shake his head, sad and slow. *Ain't so bad* he say finally, but not like he mean it.

He's unwrappin' his gum, and he shifts his weight and fishes in another pocket, brings out a bottle of water. I realize how thirsty I am and wait for him to offer me some, but he doesn't. Instead, he unscrews the bottle top and balances it on his knee, pourin' a tiny bit of water from the bottle into the upturned cap. Then he holds the silver wrap over the cap and taps it. It ain't gum. I see a white powder sprinklin' in with the water. It's like I ain't in the room no more.

Mum says you sent letters I blurt, *but I ain't seen any of 'em. Jus' the last one, the one you typed the address on.*

He don't say nothin'. Fishes round in his pocket again, brings out a plastic packet. He tears open the end of the packet without even lookin' at me. I say *Are you goin' to help us? We got a fight on our hands.*

He sighs impatiently and shoots me a cold look, like I'm the biggest disappointment he could ever have had, and my heart is back in my throat. Like when I looked over the ledge of the lift shaft, about to see Rachid and Andy get taken. I'm feelin' all <u>choked</u>.

Dad?

He tosses the end of the packet aside, sticks his fingers in and brings out a syringe.

My mouth won't register what my eyes is seein'. *You goin' to help us, Dad? Join us?*

I look at his face, and I'm rememberin' the photo that I hid under my mattress all this time, but it's like my brain is takin' a brand-new picture of him, here and now. Image burnin' itself right into my retina. Cruel.

Sabre is whinin' behin' the door, remindin' me we got battle lines drawn. It is time to go.

You goin' to join <u>me</u>? Dad spits. *I got the best protection you can get. Good stuff. Bug-proof.*

He has depressed the syringe so it's sucked up all the water and the white powder and he bunches his fist, settin' his jaw tight, like he psyching himself to punch somebody out. But there ain't nobody around to punch, only me. He ain't lookin' at me though I ain't there any more. He starin' at the back of his fist like it the most amazin' thing in the universe. Then he put the needle to the skin and he forces it in.

Dad rolls his eyes over to a old wine bottle gatherin' dust on the floor. He dips his other hand in his pocket and produces one of them multi-purpose knives, flicks up the corkscrew. He loses his grip. It slips from his fingers to the desktop. *Least have a drink wi' me...*

I'm laughin'. Wine bottle ain't even got a cork or a top. It filled with a yellow liquid that don' look like wine. I snatch up the pocket knife, wantin' to cut somethin'. I hack at the tabletop. Pathetic.

I think about the police. Compo burstin' through right now, laughin' his laugh and sayin' *Told you.*

Told you.

Compo too much respectable to discover the Attic Office. Discoverin' this den take a <u>criminal mentality</u>.

I look back at Dad's face. But his eyes ain't focused on anythin' in particular. I ain't there. The room ain't even there. And my dad ain't there.

My nose throbbin' from when I bashed it on the stairs, my guts are all mushed up and my eyes are blurrin'.

Forcin' myself to focus, get real, but when I do, all I can see is the needle stickin' out of the back of his hand. The rest of him is gone.

Payback

I sit and look at him for a while. My dad. First up, his eyes are still open, but unfocused, like he don't even know, or care, where he is. Well blissed.

You never answered my question. How long you been out of jail?

He still ain't answerin', is he?

How long, Dad? 'Nuff time for Mum to know you out. 'Nuff time for Sis to know. Compo too. 'Nuff time to track me down, score some gear and find yourself a shootin' gallery. To show me your new face.

His eyes are droopin' now. I heard about this. Noddin' out. Sleepy.

Yo, Dad, you go sleep, let those bedbugs feast on your juice, before we know it we gon' have block full of smackhead Megas. This your contribution, your solution?

Still ain't answerin'.

Dad?

I take out my phone. Shove it in his face. I snap him.

I ain't gonna need that crumpled old photo no more. I got this rebranded update version. Up to the minute, high def, all formats.

Thin line of drool leakin' out the corner of his mouth.

Dad?

Is that what you reckoned then? That all I'd want from you is a hit? That's all I been missin' all these years? Now we gonna bond over a shared needle? Happy days.

Dad?

His arm is restin' on the desktop, needle still stickin' out of his hand.

I wanna hit the roof. Wanna climb out, stick my head in the clouds. Listen to the voice of The Finger. Howl along. To get to the roof hatch I got to stand on the desk. To stand on the desk I got to clamber over the needle stickin' in Dad's hand.

I've had enough. Whole room smells of toxication.

All the same, I check all the windows firmly closed. Keep the bugs at bay. Not that they gonna want to suck any of his polluted juice anyway. If they did, they be Oh Dearin' all over the place.

I'm outta here.

Stumblin' down the stairwell like a total meth-head, zigzaggin' from one wall to the next. With my mutt, my right-hand man. *Good boy!* Praisin' him. Maybe he wasn't jus' runnin' scared from the bugs. Maybe he was guidin' me to see what I had to see. Give the dog a bone.

Vision gone fuzzy like old-school, bent-aeriel TV. Goin' down two steps at a time, three steps, back up one, fists knucklin' the peelin' paintwork.

Movement out the corner of my eye, on the wall. One of Mr B's old red cushions, for me rest my head for a minute.

Hah.

Give each other the evils. I see its antenna twitchin', like it figurin' whether or not we met before. Did we hang together back in the day?

It turns, starts to pitter-pat away, slow and easy. Bug is full, had its dinner, not interested.

Neither am I. We make our way down together, me and my mutt on the steps, bug on the wall. Companionable. Nobody about. All indoors, watchin' *Eastenders*, eatin' their grub. Sittin' roun' like a proper family.

Dad's knife is bashin' against my butt, in my pocket, annoyin' me, windin' me up deliberately, down one floor, down another – bash bash on my bum, requestin' trouble.

I stop, take it out of my pocket and pull out the corkscrew. I slam the bug in the head. Starts tuggin' backwards with its legs, strugglin' to pull away. I twist it proper, roun' and roun' like it goin' into a real cork. Screw you. I put my eyes up to the bug's head, so's I can gaze at its dyin' eyes. I'm watchin' its bloaty bodysack tryin' to reverse out of trouble, nasty legs wigglin' and scrattin' against the paint. It ain't

goin' nowhere. I keep twistin' the corkscrew till the
bug head screwed right to the wall. When it finally
stop wigglin' I tug the corkscrew straight out, see the
sweet red wine spurtin'. The bug fall to the floor with
a <u>plop</u>.

How many more floors down? I keep seein' Megas
out the corner of my eye, but when I look proper they
ain't there.

Dreamin' up different ways to slay them Megas.
More ways I can think of, the sweeter it gets.

My phone buzzes. Sis. *Yeah, wassup?*

*Your mum's back. She's safe. Compo's with her and
your bro.*

I'm heading back to my house like a shot. *Where
Big Auntie?* I demand. *We got to get organized.*

She on her way say Sis. *Her text ain't sayin' much,
but I'm feelin' she's comin' good for us.*

You sure?

No. But she Big Auntie. Gotta trust her.

I hang up. Nex' thing, I'm at my house. I wanna
see my mum.

House Cleaning

Compo don' say a word to me as I march into our kitchen. He jus' nod at Mum, step up and leave.

Connor is in the living room she say, *with strict instructions to stay there until we go in for him. Why don't you shut your dog in there too.*

Since when was Sabreboy <u>your dog</u>? He <u>our</u> dog. He Sabes, silly ol' sof'ness in the middle of our family.

You shut all the windows? I demand.

She sigh. *Yes.* She close her eyes in irritation. *I shut all the windows.* She open her eyes again and her face soften. *Look at you* she say, *you gashed your nose—*

It's nothin'.

She pauses. *Officer Cotton* she begins, *told me everythin'.*

That's nice of him.

I say *So I'm in trouble again?*

She shake her head, slow, oh so slow. *No* she say, *I owe you an apology.*

She look up at me.

Can't read her eyes. *What?*

I'm sorry she says.

At last.

Mum plonks me in front of the little bathroom mirror, dabbin' my nose with antiseptics like I am just a littl'un. She doin' it to fix my nose, or to say sorry for bein' so mad with me?

We positioned in front of the mirror in that weird way that I can see her face in it, and she see my face in it, both at the same time. So we both starin' at the bathroom mirror, watchin' each other's shiftin' moods. But neither one of us can see ourselves.

We got to be quick, Mum. Big Auntie goin' to want us all together.

Is what Officer Cotton said <u>really</u> true? Big Auntie needs to provide a lot of answers to a lot of questions.

She <u>still</u> doesn't believe about the giant bugs.

And <u>I</u> haven't told her about my seein' Dad.

I'm thinkin' the more confused one of us looks, the more hurt the other one gets. She doin' a thorough job cleanin' my nose good and proper, but it stings with the antiseptics, like pain is part of healin'.

Oww!

You should have taken more care...

I'm thinkin' of Dad sittin' in the Attic Office, all blissed out, how much it'd hurt him bad if Mum made a go at gettin' him healed up. Too much hurt to bear, I bet.

Mum I say—

No. She cut me off. *It's OK. I know enough, for*

now. Let's focus on being safe.

I'm bustin' with impatience, but then Mum add
I been discussin' the situation with Officer Cotton.

Oh. The situation. Dad? The Megas? The fightin'?
I gaze at her face in the mirror, try and read her
firm expression. Stickin' out from the bottom of the
mirror, I see a couple of antennas, quiverin' slightly
but you can tell they makin' an effort to keep still.
Very still.

Sticky-out antennas the only flaw in the Megabug
games of hide-n-seek.

I look at Mum's eyes, wonderin' if she ready for
this. I think she is. Her eyes in the mirror fix their
gaze back at me, unwaverin'.

I got my mother's eyes I think. And I bring Dad's
knife out of my back pocket and I hurl it at the
mirror.

Mirror shatters. My face and Mum's face fracture
into the sink below, razor-sharp teardrops, ripplin'
beneath the taps.

On the wall, the giant bug crouches, uncovered.

My mum's eyes rest themselves on the naked bug.
Its blood-drop eyes fix themselves back at her.

Bug moves almost faster than my eyes can follow.
Up the wall, across the ceilin', above me and Mum. It
drops, proboscis pointed between Mum's eyes.

I am ready.

My hands shoot up, catch the bug, fingers gettin'
a grip around the edge of its shell. Its front legs

wiggle and scratch at my arms, claws tryin' to slice an artery. Its head rocks backwards and forwards like movin' to a Grime track, try and manoeuvre its proboscis to pierce my skin, give me the paralysis. The nozzle tappin' against my flesh like a drumstick, but angle ain't right for it to make a puncture.

I throw the bug into the toilet. Mum slam down the lid. I flush. We look at each other for a moment, listenin'. Flush is good and long.

I see two hooks stickin' out from under the seat, grippin' tight to the sides of the bowl. Mega ain't goin' down the drain without a fight.

The cistern begin it slow refillin' process.

Mum grab hold of the toilet brush, lift up the seat and start to hammer the Mega with the brush. She bashin' it on its head, on its back, but it will not release its grip on the rim of the toilet bowl.

I grab a bottle of bleach. Twist the lid but it jus' go roun' and roun', will not unscrew.

Child-proof say Mum.

Oh yeah. <u>Squeeze</u> and twist.

I pour the bleach over the shell of the Mega. Mum is bashin' away at it with the toilet brush. Bug is startin' to crack. I pour the bleach on its head, in its eyes, but still it hangs on. Mum snaps its knee joints. The exoskeleton shatters.

I flush again. The bug washes down with the swirl of water.

The smell of bleach remains in the air. We are clean.

Decorating

There's a hammerin' at the door, and I hear Sis callin'
my name. Somethin' up.

I help Mum to her feet and she give me the
tightest hug. She ain't hugged me for as long as I
can remember. I made her stop that stuff an age ago
when it got embarrassin'. My head higher than hers
and it feel all wrong. I 'member when I was Connor's
age, always wrappin' my arms round her waist,
leanin' my head against her belly, feelin' her warmth.
Right now, I oughta push her away, but I can't let her
go. Like I'm big, and small, both at the same time.

Marsh! Sis hammerin' at the door. *Marsh!*

I look at Mum.

You see what she wants she tells me. *I'll watch
Connor.*

I ain't sure. *Are you safe?*

I am now she answer. *Do what you got to do, but
come back quick. Phone me.*

I am filled with reluctance.

From the door, Sis yells *It's Mustaph! He ain't
turned up. We got to check him!*

OK. I turn to go. *I'll be quick.*

And careful.

Careful I say, *is my middle name.*

Seconds later, me and Sis racin' down the stairs.

She peerin' at me. *Marsh? You all right?*

I'm ... I'm ... I'm jus' tired, Sis, is all. Come, let us find Muskrat. Gather ourselves.

Sis don't look too certain about my all-rightness, but you know what? What's all right? Who's all right? Somebody tell me that. Anybody?

So Sis start deliverin' a lecture on all fresh things she found about the bugs, but I ain't listenin'. I figure I know everythin' I need to know, which is all the best ways to splatter the suckers.

You _sure_ you all right? she ask.

I met my dad.

Ah. She stops lecturin' and gives my arm a squeeze. I feel her fingers round the back of my arm, firm, and her thumb jus' restin' by my shoulder. It's like she got good vibes floodin' into me through that thumb. She could rest it there for ever. All would be well.

Sis is overjoyed to see three Megas, lurkin' around a corner. I don't like it. If they sittin' in open view now, how many goin' to come out when it _really_ dark? But Sis see a perfec' opportunity for target practice, whip out her precious nail gun and _kapow!_ she crucifixin' them bugs to the wall.

*One of these suckers has
its fill with you she say, that
about a litre, maybe a fifth of
what you got in total.*

I ain't really listenin'. I got severe nail gun envy.

*Two of the suckers, that be leavin' you driftin' in
and out of wakeyness.*

Should have rummaged back of that van myself,
coulda fixed myself some interestin' hardware.
'Lectric drill – send them Megas spinnin' and
splattin' all over the shop.

*Three of 'em take their fill, boy, you ain't wakin' up
again. You get me? They taken more'n half of what
you got. Not enough lef' bother keep pumpin' roun'.
You flatlinin' for sure. You listenin', Mallow?*

Nope.

We get to Mustaph's place, knock on the door.

No answer.

We knock again. Still no answer.

I'm sweatin'. *Break it down* I say. *Bash it in!*

Calm yourself. She turn to me. *Do your countin'
trick.*

Sis! This ain't the time—

This exackly the time. Count. She fixin' me stern.
To ten. Do it.

I'm sighin', but I surrender 'cos I know there no
point arguin' with her. *Mega One* I begin. *Mega Two.*
Nice and slow. *Mega Three, Mega Four...*

I count all the way to Mega Ten and there still

ain't no answer from Mustaph. *All right – can we bash it down now?*

Sis turn the handle and push the door open. I feel the fool. We step in.

Place looks ghostly without Muskrat's family all sittin' there watchin' the TV.

He ain't here I whisper.

Let's jus' check the boy's room. Sis is whisperin' too. Like we got some secret. The secret is us. We don't want them to hear us.

Push open the door to Mus's den, and place in darkness, as usual.

Mus?

Hey, boy, you awake?

No sound.

Mus?

I hear a rustlin' sound from where his tent is, like he's turnin' over in his sleepin' bag.

He be nappin' again. Even now.

That boy got zzzs for brains.

I take a step towards the curtains, put some light on the subject.

I hear the <u>pitter-pat</u>.

Don't move say Sis.

Don't worry, I ain't movin'.

I get the feelin' we bein' watched.

<u>Pitter-pat. Pitter-pat.</u>

You know what? I'm sick of this. Every time I come and visit Muskrat it's like walkin' straight into

a horror movie. Boy don't
even know how irritatin'
it is.

   Hold up I whisper to Sis.
I reach my hand out towards his bust of
Beethoven. Right about now, I ain't too much of a
enthusiast about feelin' around in the dark in case
I find myself twizzlin' some creepy-crawly whiskers.
But my fingers find the night-vision goggles, and I
snap 'em off of that ol' decomposer and fit 'em onto
my own head.

   I'm instantly wishin' that I hadn't of done that.
Sincerely.

   If there's one thing creepier than seein' a mob of
Megas in the day, it's seein' them in the darkness.
Mustaph's tent is no longer a tent. It is a crawlin'
mass of giant bedbugs. You can't even <u>see</u> the tent.
Them Megas coverin' every last inch, creepin' and
probin' and <u>pitter-pattin'</u>. In the middle of it all must
be Mustapha.

   Sis, do not move a muscle.

   I turn my head and see her face in the green
murk of night vision. She is as still as a old game of
Grandma's Footsteps, but the look on her face is like
she made a big mess in her pants. I'm thinkin' my
pants goin' to join in solidarity.

   What do I do, Sis?

   She hiss back *I can't see a thing, how should I
know what you do? What's goin' on, Marsh?*

You don't wanna know.

Am I goin' to find out?

Get your nail gun ready to do some serious firin'.
Soon as I give us some light.

She don't answer, but I see her gulp and I take
that as an affirmative.

Turn the goggles towards the tent. Bugs don't seem
to realize we here, focusin' on pokin' their proboscises
through the canvas. I take two steps, steady and slow,
in the direction of Mustaph's curtains.

Now!

I pull open the curtains. Light floods into the
room. All them Megas give a jolt. A hundred bug eyes
jerk in our direction, antennas instantly stiffenin'.

Like I say, Sis be the fearless one. She straight
away fire off three shots from the nail gun, right into
the shells of three of them bugs. Nails pass straight
through 'em like sheets of paper.

Oww! Aaagh! from inside the tent.

Damn. You can only be nailin' them bugs if you
got somethin' to nail 'em to. Those bits of metal
goin' straight through the bugs, straight through
the canvas, and givin' poor ol' Muskrat the rudest
awakenin'.

As one, the bugs pitter-pat towards us – fast
when they ain't laden down with other people's
blood. Proboscises is twitchin' like crazy. Dinner jus'
presented itself to these fellas.

I ain't thinkin' my pocket knife goin' to be much

use at this point. I kick
away couple of bugs already
attached themselves to my
footwear. Luckily, my hands
thinkin' a little faster than
my brain, reachin' straight out towards the tabletop
where Mus store his spray paint. I toss a can in
Sis's direction.

Decorate!

Kickin' off a couple more Megas, I grab a can
of my own. In fact I grab a can for each hand. I
suddenly found I'm ambidexterous.

Let us spray.

Blaaam! These critters do not like aerosol one
bit. Soon as the spray hittin' 'em they wigglin' like
poison goin' straight through their pores. I'm firin'
Tibetan Gold and Deep Ivy, and it mos' definitely
must be said, them bugs look more fun covered in
this new colour scheme. Sis is sprayin' Shocking
Pink, which really suits 'em. They love it so much
they turnin' on their backs and wagglin' their little
legs in glee. Not.

Ohhhh, owwww, ooooh screamin' Mustaph from
inside the tent. *Murdah! Murdahhh!*

Insectoid panic. I'm seein' a dozen or more bugs
squeezin' through one crack in the ceilin', and at
least as many more ziggerzag behind our legs and
weasel under the gap between the door and floor.
Loads more scramble behind Mustaph's wardrobe.

They tryin' to slide themselves into every hidin' place they can find. Within seconds, we left with a couple of dozen technicolour bug corpses scattered on the floor. Not quite dead – wigglin' in death throes. But the rest have vanished. It's like they wasn't even here. Devious suckers.

There's a rippin' sound, and the zip to the tent unfastens and out hops one 'ceedingly awake Muskrat. Never seen him move so fast. He sound like somebody repeatedly stabbin' him with a red-hot poker. He literally hoppin' mad, but that partly explained by the big nail he got stickin' into the sole of his foot. He got one more stickin' out his thigh and a third one gripped in his fist, which he wavin' at us in a highly accusatory manner. *What you doin', man! What you doin'! You murderin' me in my bed!*

He stops cussin' us out when he see the bedbug carnage scattered around him. But is he grateful to his brave saviours?

Ohh, man! Mus clutchin' his head like the end of the world just occurred before his very eyes. *My can of Tibetan Gold! What have you done with it? You know how hard it is to get hold of that shade?*

Like I say, Muskrat don't live in the same universe as the rest of us.

Sis is concentratin' on her phone. She had a message.

Come on she look up at us, *none of us safe here.*

Let's get you fixed up. Then we got to all hook up together. That a message from Big Auntie. She callin' a meetin'. Down in the Community Room. Says she's been assemblin' defences.

My eyes pop out my head. *You mean she finally believe?*

Sis smile. *It Big Auntie. She never <u>dis</u>believe us. She like me. She gotta make certain she sure of things. Well, she is sure of things now. It goin' to be a long and bloody night.*

Bravery Bled All Over the Carpet

I'm on my phone tellin' Mum Mustaph had a little accident. She know all about first aid, from back in the day, she work at the hospital. She makin' her way down.

So what you doin creepin' round my place anyway? says Mus.

What <u>you</u> doin' sleepin' in your bed, when the whole Finger under attack? I say.

Hard work, tryin' to prise my folks away from the TV. I was enjoyin' a power nap, yeah?

Yeah?

Sis says *Your leg is lookin' proper nasty. Marsh, what your mum say? Think she can do somethin' with these wounds?*

Yeah, but this lookin' bad. We ought to call a ambulance, get him to the hospital.

Ain't goin' to no hospital say Mus. *Full of sick people.*

Bad plan anyway adds Sis. *We go off to the hospital we ain't goin' to be doin' no good here. We needed at the meetin'. We better take a look at your wounds ourselves.*

Mustaph feeds me a worried glance. I get it, can't help but laugh. *We goin' to have to get your trousers off to get at the wound, boy.*

Sis giggle. *Don't worry, Musky. I seen it all before.*

First up I say, *we got to remove the nails in order to get your trousers off.* I grab hold of the nail stickin' outta Mustaph's thigh. It is well stuck. *Got any pliers?*

Under normal circumstances, that would be a stupid question, but this is Mustaph's room we're talkin' about.

Sis fetch me the pliers and I use 'em to get a good solid grip. I say *This is goin' to really hurt.*

Thanks very—

I yank.

Mustaph scream like he bein' murdered.

Easy, boy say Sis. She got her arms roun' his shoulder, holdin' him firm.

One down I say, *one to go.*

Whoa, hold up, hold up say Mus, his eyes widenin' in panic. *This don't feel right, don't feel right at all.* He looks confused. *I wet myself.*

He got a wet patch spreadin' across his trouser leg, sure enough.

Damn say Sis. *He ain't wet himself.* She puts

her fingers to his leg. She turns her palm. She got red prints.

Damn I also say.

What goin' on? What happenin', man?

I'm sorry, Mus I say, *I just unplugged the wound.*

What!

Quick say Sis, *get his trousers off.*

What?

Pullin' Mustaph's trousers down is easy 'cos he so skinny and they so baggy. Also easy to avoid bashin' the nail still stickin' out the bottom of his foot. But his thigh is a bloody mess. The nail hole ain't too big, but blood is pourin' out like somebody just switched on a tap.

We need some towels I say. *We makin' a mess.*

A shadow looms over me. *You're making a mess all right.*

We all look up. *Mum.*

Mustaph force a smile and say *Am I goin' to die?*

No she say. *Like my son said, you're just makin' a mess on your floor. Sis!* She clap her hands, focus Sis's attention. *Clean towels from the bathroom. Quick as you can.*

Mum shoot me a look, let me know she is in control. She bend down close to Mustaph, open up the first-aid kit she brought with her.

If I ain't dyin' says Mustaph, *then how come I'm bleedin' so much?*

Don't be such a baby she say. *Your friend hit you*

*in a vein is why. You should
be glad the nail didn't pierce
an artery.*

His eyes get wider still.
*How do you know it's not
an artery?*

*Mustapha, if she'd hit an
artery, we wouldn't be having this
conversation. You'd be unconscious.*

While she's talkin', she's cleanin' the wound
and she is right, it ain't hardly nothin'. I reckon
Mustapha is a wuss.

Mum applies a dressin', presses down
against the wound, and the blood is
beginnin' to slow down.

This be the point where you cheer up the
patient with a joke, so I say *Hey, boy, at least the
Megabugs ain't goin' to try and get you now. You lost
so much blood, you ain't got nothin' left to quench a
gnat's thirst.*

Sis, Mustaph and Mum all stare at me in a highly
unamused fashion.

What about the nail stickin' out of my foot?
ask Musk.

Mum peers close, puts her fingers on it. *It isn't
anything. It is much the same as if you stepped on a
drawing pin.*

Oh, that's good—

What's that over there? Mum point at the wall.

Mustaph looks.

She yanks.

Mustaph scream like he bein' murdered. Again.

You children say Mum, *you like to pretend you are so tough. Where is your real bravery?*

My real bravery just bled all over the carpet.

We all smile.

Is he goin' to need a hospital? asks Sis.

I look out the window. Last of the light is fadin'.

Mum shake her head. *We've got an emergency meeting just starting. Can you hobble?*

Oh yeah say Mus. *I been practisin' all my life.*

Chainsaw Envy

We can hear people of The Finger
filin' past Mustaph's flat, makin' their
way down to the meetin', or draggin' wheelie
bags packed with essentials, makin' their
escape.

We got to go I say to Mum.

Time runnin' out. She dash up to get
Connor and Sabre. Me and Sis play nursemaid
to our feeble friend.

Five minutes later, my family steppin' out,
together, make our way to the big meetin'. I ain't
never seen the stairwell so busy with life. Mums
carryin' babes in their arms, kids wieldin' cricket
bats and fryin' pans, gangs of men with knives,
hammers, guns. Bugs doin' well to keep a low profile,
they ain't goin' to fare so well in a straight-up clash
with mobs from The Finger.

As we make our way down among the mix of
battlers and evacuees I see a couple of Megas been
caught out under the harsh light of the stairwell –
what left of them. I begin to feel hope in my heart.

Me and Mum ain't sayin' much. Feels like we said so much already, without the need for words. She keepin' Connor under her wing, and I got Sabretooth on a improvised piece of string. We all goin' to stick together now.

Mus is on crutches that Mum magicked up for him when she went for my bro and my dog. He is in better spirits.

Everybody all a buzz.

Community Room on the first floor, little more than a bare hall, furnished with wonky wooden chairs and decorated by murals of kids' games, of a artistic quality like they been painted by the kids themselves. We grab ourselves some seats. Hall contain about one hundred citizens and lined with beefy men look like they work as bouncers or bailiffs. Look like they squash giant bugs in their spare time, for fun. So, you know, place has quite a pleasant atmosphere. First time in a while people feel safe, get me?

Hush fall across the room, people turn their heads, stare at a figure marchin' down the aisle like there's a serious beef need settlin', carryin' – I kid you not – a chainsaw. Chainsaw is switched on, blade runnin' round like a rabid dog, motor growlin' with teeth-shakin' menace. Teeth of the saw already clotted with bits of bug leg, schnozzles and squashed cherry eyes. This is Big Auntie, her steel-capped boots thuddin' with authority as she make her way to the front.

Never mind the nail gun, now I got serious

chainsaw envy.

Behind her is Compo,
tryin' to look self-important,
but comin' across as a fat-
belly weasel. Troop of six
minders marchin' either
side of them, make Compo
seem wimpier still.

They get to the front. Big
Auntie turn to face us, switch off
the chainsaw to speak. Applause
breaks out.

Good evenin' to you all Big
Auntie begin. *I shall keep this
short. Most of us have now seen
first-hand the menace we facin' here in
The Finger. Apologies owed to the youth among
us who worked so hard to put the word out, and
were doubted. That doubt – disbelief – still exists
with authorities on the outside, as Officer Cotton
will attest.*

Here she give a nod towards Compo, who open
his mouth to begin his own speech, but she talk over
him. *We got a team, even as I speak, workin' on tryin'
to persuade the council and the police to come in and
give us the assistance, the protection we need. But
lackin' that, we got to protect ourselves.*

Murmur of approval passes through the crowd.
Hands lift high, bearin' weapons of 'stonishin'

range and imagination. Big Auntie looks us over approvingly.

She holds up her hand, callin' for silence once more. *Lot of families already upped and left. That is good. Sensible thing to do, especially those with littl'uns. If you got any place to go: <u>please!</u> Go! Quick as you can, no messin'.*

But some of us ain't got nowhere to go to. Some of us ain't got no wherewithal to go where we want to go. Some of us invalid, bed-bound, and the council ain't left us with no lift with which to move ourselves. Some of us can't go stay with our family, our cousins, on account of our cousins bein' on the eleventh floor, our uncles bein' on the eight floor, our in-laws bein' three flats over to our left. The Finger the only place we got.

But we are all here for each other. Those of us that ain't in Fightin' Patrols, lock yourselves in, in large groups. Be strong together. Lock your windows. Block your letter boxes. Keep your eyes peeled and make sure there's always at least one of you wide awake! Remember: safety in numbers. Ain't nobody else here for us, so our families, our friends, our neighbours are all we have. We just got to make it through the night.

Meantime, we keep tryin' to bring in the outside help. Here she lower her voice, show she got somethin' heavy to lay on us. *But let me show you, even now, what we up against.*

She thrust out her hand,
holdin' out her phone. Swing
it wide so whole audience
get to see, like this the mos'
dramatic weapon in the world.
See this? she declare. *This is
the only protection we been given
... Council Emergency 24-Hour Phoneline.
Officer Cotton?* She turn to Compo, give him
his moment of importance. He happily takes
the phone from her. She say *I dialled that 24-
hour number. Tell us, Officer, what response
do you hear?*

Compo holds the phone to his ear,
listens close. He says *Lines are closed
after 5.00 p.m.!*

Chorus of boos fills the room. First time
in his life Compo heard boos that ain't aimed at
him. Big smile slide across his chops.

Big Auntie turns to face him. *Officer Cotton,
what've you got to say about that? Tell me what
your own colleagues got to offer us.*

He coughs, try and bring himself together. *I am
sad to report* he says, *that my superior officers at
the police station were not prepared to accept the
evidence that I personally captured and took to the
station. Indeed, they actually laughed when I showed
them an example of a giant bug proboscis.*

Shame! somebody call out.

Big Auntie has served him a perfect ball. I ain't sure whether she kind-hearted or cruel-minded. All Comp gotta do is hit his home run.

So basically he conclude, *it's just us, on our own. Er, but we're in it together. You, me and the youth of The Finger, united against our common enemy!*

Cheers all round. Man is beamin' like this the best day of his life.

Big Auntie steps forward again. She take a deep breath and her voice booms through the room. *We got strength in numbers, solidarity. Tell me the truth now, if you was to place bets on who still be runnin' around by mornin' – us or the giant bugs – who would you put your money on?*

The Fingerrr! someone yells out.

Several others echo the sentiment. *The Fingerrr!*

Big Auntie joins the enthusiastic answer by revvin' up the chainsaw. Its roar fills the room. *The Finger has stood up against worse!*

Big Auntie ain't called Big Auntie for nothin'.

We whoop and we cheer. This feel sweet. This is everythin' I been waitin' for.

So this is the plan. She feed us her mos' serious face. *We have set up a roamin' posse of Mega-splatters. We got twenty of 'em, primed to split into assault groups of five. And we got guard groups to look out for those who can't defend themselves. Group leaders tell everyone their mobile numbers. We all hooked up. And we are tooled up.*

Sis turn to me and
say *True. We got 'nuff
weapons to fill an entire
Crimewatch series. Bugs
ain't got no chance. We be
the Neighbourhood Watch
from Hell.*

Oh Dear

Ten minutes later, we all gathered in our livin' room
– me, Mum, Con, Sis, and Mustaph, nice 'n' cosy on
a pile of cushions, Mus's bad leg levered up onto a
dinin' chair. I ain't hardly seen him look happier.

Big Auntie drop in on us, give us one final check
before lock-down. Connor shuffle nervously by Mum's
side. Mum strokin' his head. Big Auntie gesture
towards me with her chainsaw. *Young man, you a
lucky boy, 'cos you got your big brother Marshall
O'Connor lookin' out for you. Ain't no one tougher,
or braver.*

I'd be a bit tougher and braver if she'd let me
have use of her chainsaw. But I can tell she ain't
relinquishin' <u>that</u> for no one.

Mus look more like a invalid than a soldier,
on account of bein' all patched up where he got
accidentally nail-gunned. But he's brought along his
spray cans, now we know we can use them as extra-
lethal bug spray. And my hound Sabretooth is puttin'
on his bravest face.

Our task is to keep each other safe and protect six

of the littl'uns, kids of
the Mega-splatter Posse.
Posses made up of a mix of
dads and mums – some of the
women are fiercer than the
men, yeah? Kids are settled in
mine and Con's room, which has
been checked and quadruple-checked
for bug access. Even so, we goin' to take
turns sentryin' through the night. Right
now, the littl'uns all glued to a selection of
DVDs we set for 'em. Best way to keep 'em
awake, innit?

Me and mine can take care of each
other. This night is goin' to pass, easy
and safe.

So this is us, five brave warriors and our dog
all mobbed together in the livin' room. Sofa pull
out into one of them sofa beds, Mum and Con-
Con sharin', and I bagsied the big armchair, as I
am the eldest male of the house. Mustaph lyin' in
his sickbed of cushions like a pampered princess. Sis
wrapped in a sleepy bag.

Let's play some games says Mum. She don' look
like she in the mood for games. Her face is grey. She
can't leave her phone alone. She give Con-Con her
biggest, fakest smile.

Cool say Con-Con, snatchin' up his game controller.

No, no, no. She shake her head. *Together. People games.*

Con-Con screw his face up into big frown, as if to say *You is surely insane?*

Mustaph say *I 'member we used to play this game where you have to say name of a animal, like rabbit, and the next person has to say a animal beginnin' with the last letter of rabbit, tortoise for example. Next person has to say a 'e' animal, and it keep goin' until person can't think of no animal that hasn't already been said, then they out.*

Let's play that one! say Con.

Is Muskrat serious? We maybe all goin' to die tonight. He ain't even fakin' it, like Mum.

But we got to put on a brave face, for my bro if nothin' else. *What about that game where you got to answer the questions, but you ain't allowed to say yes or no. What about that?* I say.

Mustaph shrug. *Whatevs.*

Sis, I notice, is watchin' the walls. She is watchin' the door. She is watchin' the windows. Her eyes do not settle. We blocked up everythin' we could think of, try and stop them Megas bustin' in. But me and Sis both know they sneaky.

We start the game. Mum looks at me and she say *Am I the most beautiful mum in the world?*

She always try and catch me on that one. When we was little I'd of said *Mummy, you the mos' delicious mum in the whole of everywhere!*

I give her a look and
say *Mum, you know the
answer.*

She smile at me, and I turn
to Con-Con, and I say *Poo! Bro,
did you just poo-poo your pants?*

Oh yeah, man, the number of
times I caught him on that one. But
he extra focused this evenin', and he
say *I mos' certainly did not.*

Con turn to Mustapha, sneaky look on
his face and say *I bet you dirtied your pants
when you found all them bugs coverin'
your tent?*

Without thinkin', Mus goes *No!* like it
the biggest insult in the world.

Con in hysterics, rollin' roun', clappin'
his hands. *You out, you fool! You ain't
supposed to say that word!*

Mustaph tut and cross his arms in a sulk.
What a donut, gettin' caught out by my idiot
brother, first go too.

I'm listenin'. Listenin' hard. Do I hear a
pitter-pat?

Then Con turn to Sis and he say *I bet you're glad
you didn't make no stupid mistake like that?*

In my own head I hear it, that's all. I am so wiped.
Feel a black sleep creepin' down on me.

Sis ain't no fool to fall for that trick of Con's. But

she can see Mustaph been put in a deep mood for bein' so outwitted. Kind as ever, she catch my eye – just for a sec – and answer my bro *Yes, I am.*

Con-Con shriekin' with delight. *You're out! Out! Oh, you guys are rubbish at this.*

But Sis jus' bein' the diplomat. She stand up, go and peek in at the littl'uns.

Now Connor turn to Mum and ask *Mum, who is the best-lookin', me or Mushface?*

My brother is a idiot. *Yo, fool! You got to ask a question that got a yes or no answer.*

Immediately he point his stinky finger at me and yell *Hey, Mum, Marshall loses – he just said yes and no!*

That's cheatin', Con. You know that don't count!
Yes, it do!

Then I look at Mum and point my own finger at Con. *There, Mum! He's out as well, 'cos he jus' said yes!*

Mum laugh, rollin' on her side into Con-Con. *I guess I'm the winner.* She raise both arms in the air like boxin' champ. *As ever!*

But, you know, I ain't had no sleep since night before yesterday. Sabretooth got his hairy head nuzzled in my lap, soft and warm. Dog sleepier than me. I'm feelin' my eyelids startin' to pull the wool over my eyeballs. Mum ask me a question that I ain't hearin', and she come kneel down next to me, stroke my hair. *Marshy?*

I force my lids open.
We are sittin' in danger.
My eyelids weigh heavier
than borin' old school books.
*Marshy, why don't you let
yourself get some sleep? You've
already been a hero for us. Let
someone else take first watch duty.*

My eyes open wide. *Oh. And what
happen when them Megabugs come?*

Mum waggle her rollin' pin front of my
eyes. *They come, we start splattering. And
we'll yell out for you to wake, straight away.
I promise.*

*Mum, Connor ain't goin' to be able to watch
himself. He too young.*

Boy come dive-bombin' across the room,
throwin' Jackie Chan shapes, and makin'
the mos' horrible racket, like it prove he can
demolish a dozen of them monsters with his
bare hands.

Bugs gonna eat you alive, boy Mus tell him,
helpfully.

But Mum sittin' there strokin' my head, nice and
soft. She half lift, half walk me across to my room,
slip me beneath the duvet of my bed.

She say *I'll take first watch.*

Sound of cartoon movie <u>biff bam bangin</u>' aroun'
the room. Kids eatin' crisps.

'S a nice room.

Mum, strokin' away. Me, feelin' them heavy school books drawin' a veil over my wakefulness. *Don't you worry, Marshy, we're all watchin' for each other. You sleep easy now.*

Oh, it's nice.

Yeah…

I'm awake!

How long I been out? Clock on the wall say 4.15. What?

I look across the room. A scatterin' of littl'uns, propped against the wall on Con-Con's bed, snuggled in sleepin' bags across the floor like little caterpillars, sprawled across a bean bag like a discarded doll. Rugrats everywhere. What a sleepover.

Over by the door, slumped in a chair from the kitchen, my little bro. He asleep on duty.

I got a moment panic. Asleep on duty! But Connor ain't got no Megabug slurpin' away at him. Ain't none of the other littl'uns either.

Con I whisper, so as to wake him, but not the rugrats. Too soft, ain't no noise at all from my mouth. *Con!* a little louder. Still ain't no noise.

Got to sit up, get up, go and wake him. Yo, I am tired. My arms and legs just ain't havin' none of this wakin' business. Maybe I'll jus' keep watch myself, from here, horizontal guard duty.

Out the corner of my eye, I see movement.

Oh yeah, it's me.
My legs, startin'
to wake. And my arms,
beneath the duvet.

I am weird.

What is my limbs up to under
there? Be still.

They won't!

Put my hands up to my cheek in
freakiness.

They ain't at my cheek. They didn't come.
They still under the duvet, movin' in weird
rhythm. What am I doin' under there? Pull
up my hands.

My hands won't move.

What is movin'?

Con! I yell. *Con!*

There is no sound. My tongue is asleep in
my mouth. My jaw glued shut.

CONNOR!

Please, no. Please please please, no.

Roll my eyeballs down at the duvet, four lumps
under there, ain't me.

Listen.

Slurp.

Please, no!

CONNOR!

Slurp slurp slurp.

Shake 'em off. Shake 'em off! Shake!

Nothin'.

Shake. Shake shake shake.

Shakeshakeshakeshakeshake!

Jus' four big lumps, growin' bigger, slurpin' away.

Roll my eyeballs up to the ceilin'. Always liked lookin' at the ceilin', pretend it the sky and you flyin' high. This be the route to a different land, maybe a different planet, when I was younger, Con-Con's age. Bedroom ceilin' is sweet.

Hear the door openin'. Roll my eyes. Mum!

Mum! Mum! Help! Help me!

No sound. She smilin' across the room, and put a hand down on Con-Con's head, stroke his hair, soft. She look across at me, see my eyes open.

Awake, hey? she say to me, soft. *Your little brother was supposed to be watchin' over you for once. Always the responsible one, hey, Marshy?*

HELP ME!

Frown fall across her face. Yes! Concern. Yes!

HELP ME, MUM!

But she stare down at her toes. *I'm sorry I didn't believe you* she say. *I'm sorry I didn't trust you to make the right choices. Marsh, I promise...*

Please...

...I promise I'll never let you down again.

She kiss Con on the top of the head, smile contentedly in my direction. She is <u>never</u> goin' to come and save me. I am screamin' at her, yellin' my head off, but she jus' smile my way. *My beautiful, gorgeous son...*

I am cryin' now.
I can feel the tears cool
against my cheek.

She sees my tears. She steps
towards me. She stops. Her
jaw drops. Her eyes widen. She
lunges forward.

She pulls the duvet off of me.
We both look down.

There are four of them. One on each
arm and leg.

Me and Mum scream. I only hear hers.

I been shanked. Bug suckers in me,
flowin' red. They are fillin' themselves.

They paralyzed me. They are drinkin' me
alive. I feel cool flow of blood along my veins,
out through the puncture, up into their straws.
Now it is their blood. Now it is in them.

NOOOOOOOOOOOOOOOOOO! Mum's scream wakin'
everybody, but it does not stop the bugs from
emptyin' me.

Sis is in the doorway right away, her eyes poppin'
out of her head when she sees me on the bed gettin'
slurped.

Sabe is right next to her and his eyes pop out of
his head too. He barks, looks up at Sis, like it her job
to sort it out.

All aroun' the room, littl'uns are yellin' and screamin', their own eyes poppin' out. All of 'em starin' at me in horror.

Connor too.

They think I am bein' killed. I look down at the Megas, each one half-filled with my blood. I mus' be half empty. I feel a chill. Am I dyin', then? If I'm so cold how comes I'm sweatin' so much? How come I'm strugglin', but I'm still?

Get 'em off. Get 'em off. Get 'em off. No voice.

Got no movement, other than inside, blood flowin' outta my veins, a icy draft oozin' its way down the inside of my arms. On the outside, I am a stiff.

Oh my God Mum is sayin'. *Oh my God.* She grab one of the Megas with both hands and pull at it, tryin' to tug it off of my arm. My arm moves 'cos it's attached to the schnozzle and Mum is pullin' the Mega back. I ain't movin' my arm myself. I am a ragdoll. Mega ain't lettin' go. Sis tugs at the Mega on my leg, makes my leg jerk.

They tuggin' and I'm jerkin'. Arms and legs twitchin' all over like I am a flesh-and-blood avatar.

Sabre whinin' away. My chest hurts where my heart is. My heart is what pumps my blood but by now there ain't much left. I am Emptyin'.

Mum bashin' at the bugs with her fists but the bugs will not let go.

I won't let them take you Mum is cryin'. *I cannot lose you.*

I am a Dead-
Body Marshall.
Can't feel nothin',
jus' my heart goin'
boom.

Mum pull out Dad's army
knife from her pocket, lookin'
at it, thinkin'. I see pink mist. What
she doin'? Thinkin' for a long time. Too
long. Clock on the wall say 4.16. Prince
Marshall O'Connor the First died at 4.16
in the mornin'.

Mustaph stroll up. He only jus' woke
up? He give a big yawn, stare at the
wall behind Mum. Has a can in his hand.
He sprays. Hiss. Hiss. The room is full
of turquoise fumes. My vision hazy, like a
death fog. A Mega sneakin' up behin' Mum's
back, but Mustaph spray it turquoise. It's
wigglin' to death. Another on the wall. Mus
decorate that one too.

Mum frantic, pullin' out the knife blades, one
by one. Small blade, big blade, corkscrew where I got
the Mega in the head, scissors.

Scissors. My mum usin' her brain.

Don't wanna look. Can't help it. Mum wedges a
bug between her knees, wraps her fist round its
schnozzle, gets the scissors where the schnozzle is
stuck into me. Starts to cut.

She cuts for ever. Scissors too blunt. Dad's stupid army knife is old crock.

Sis runs in with the kitchen scissors.

Schnozzle comes away. Mum throws the bug across the room. Sabre leaps on it, and shakes it, my blood splashin' all over the carpet.

Tip of its sucker still stuck into my leg. Blood pumpin' out like a broken pipe. I'm needin' emergency plumber. I am anti-coagulated.

Mum? Wish they could hear me. Wish I could speak to them.

Mum wedgin' a second Mega between her knees, snippin' away at its sucker. Sis snippin' at the third.

Mustaph aimin' his spray can at the walls. He spray again, bright, dazzlin' colour. Bug behind Sis.

How many bugs?

Con-Con run out of the room. Leavin' me. No, no, it is me, I am leavin', pantin', pantin'. I am a hot dog. Watch my blood flowin' like the fountain in the park used to do, back in the day.

Mum?

I'm seein' rainbows.

You're in shock.

Mum has cut off the second Mega. Sabretooth waitin' to catch it like a tennis ball in the park with the dried-up fountain in a rainbow.

Breathe easy.

Sis cuts off the third. Catch, boy. Mum, I'm runnin' out of breath now because you are grey. Rainbow turn

grey. Mum jammin'
her fingers over a
sucker stem, blood
leakin' out between
her fingers. Con-Con back
in the room.

Hi, bro I say, silent. He
brought me a pack of Blu-Tack.
<u>Thoughtful</u>, yeah? Rollin' a blob
between his finger 'n' thumb like a bogey.

I wish. I wish I wasn't dyin'.

Con-Con press the Blu-Tack bogey
into the end of the scissored schnozzle.
Is a plug. My blood stop pumpin' out.
My brother the emergency plumber. Con
roll another blob of Blu-Tack, plug up the
second sucker. Mum snippin' away at the
fourth. Sabretooth is waitin' to play catch-n-
shake. Team O'Connor.

I roll my eyes. A bug sneak behind a
littl'un's head, nozzle quiverin', wonderin'
which be the juiciest part of his face to have a stab.
It turn its head for a second, like it gloatin' at me,
then turn back, aim its sucker over one of his eyes.

Movement to my right. Sis got her nail gun.
<u>Phutt!</u> The Megabug is nailed to the wall.

I see Con got one wrappin' its legs roun' his ankles.
I can't do nothin', jus' watch. Mum grabs her rollin'
pin and she smashes the smithereens out of the bug.

We are ambushed.

All our defences. All our care. Bugs jus' hid themselves away <u>inside</u> the flat while it still daylight. Watch us from their hidey-holes as we barricade ourselves in. Wait for the sleep.

Sis on her BlackBerry callin' Big Auntie's assault group. Effin' and blindin'. No time.

Mus is sprayin' at bugs on the walls. Mum smashin' 'em on the ground.

Where's the chainsaw?

I am sleepy now...

I'm awake! Everythin' upside down and bumpy-bumpy.

We out of our house. Stairwell of The Finger.

You gonna be all right, boy. Sis's voice whisperin' in my head. She got her hand on my butt, bad Sis. Bad bugs splattered along the stairwell. Con and Sabes trottin' after me, growlin' and watchin' for Megas.

Twist round my head, see Mum in front, upside down, goin' <u>whack whack</u> with her rollin' pin, makin' Mega pancake.

You gonna be all right. Sis's voice sayin' again, like I ain't gonna be all right. She carryin' me like I ain't full of no weight, because I lost four cartons of juice before I got Blu-Tack sucker corks blockin' my leakages.

Sirens I'm hearin' in my head. <u>Nee-naw nee-naw nee-naw.</u>

There's one I
say in my head,
seein' a Mega crawlin'
along the floor, reachin'
up its front legs to try and
hitch a lift on my danglin'
ears. Kapow! Sis fire off a nail
straight through its head, pin
it to the floor. Mustaph hobblin'
along, tryin' to bash their heads with
his crutches.

Another Mega, on the ceilin'. Try and
raise my finger, point. Gonna bash it.
Finger ain't movin'. Can't even lift a...
Sleepy me...

Swingin' aroun' like I am a funfair. Sis,
your arms are big and strong. Passin' me
roun' like a Pass the Parcel. Mum, you take
me, is it because I am dyin' now? Goodbye.
Love you.

Kapow! Kapow! Sis lettin' rip at those uglies.
Sis never let me have a go on the nail gun and now
I am dyin'. Everybody else gettin' to split and splat.
I'm in Mum's arms and she kiss my head. I have
nothin' left.

Big Auntie loomin' over me whizzin' and
whirrin', doin' her Texas Chainsaw Massacre. Gimme
a go, gimme...

Yahh! yell Sis. *Now they're real sorry they messed with us.*

I'm real sorry.

Down we clatter, roun' and roun'. Mum carryin' me more than Dad ever did. Down and down. Blood and shell all over the walls. Mustaph sprayin' his colours like mad Picasso, hissin' and howlin'.

My dog lickin' my ears, ticklin'.

Blood. Gallons. Everywhere. 'Cept in me.

Ground floor. Megas blockin' the escape.

Someone say *We're losin' him...*

Someone drop me to the floor like a sack of loot. No pain. Face to face with Megabug. A foot stomps down, crushes its head. Bad brains. Look up, Compo big size twelves.

Yo Comp say Sis. *You is a little late.*

Slash of chain, roar of metal. More brains. Big Auntie, flexin' her muscles.

Someone say *You'll be OK, OK?*

OK...

I see a giant bug suckin' a rat.

I'm bein' dragged along the ground. By a bug? No. Sis. Towards the exit. But Sis got a Mega attached to her leg, claws grippin' tight, steadyin' itself. Sabre snarlin' forward, sinkin' his fangs round its head. Crunch.

Sis kickin' out her leg, tryin' to get the headless Mega to release its death grip. Mustaph bat it off with a crutch. Hit it for six.

We're losin' him.
We're losin' him...

More Megas. Compo
struttin' towards them.
Oh, I see, he got a taser.

Blue lightnin'
everywhere. Bugs burnin'.
Mustaph and Con-Con whoopin'.
Sis sayin' *Go, Comp!* Compo the
brave fighter. Big Auntie swingin' her
chainsaw, hackin', choppin'.

Everybody battlin'. Everybody 'cept me.
And Mum. Mum cradlin' me.
Doors swing open. Exit The Finger.
Dragged into early mornin' air.
Someone say *Faster, faster...*
Someone say *Mess with us?*
Someone, *Monsters...*
Squealin' brakes and headlights shinin'.
The meat wagon is here. It has come for me.

Exit

I'm awake! Suffocatin', smothered! Bedbug
underbelly mufflin' my horror.

Rip off the bug with my hands but my hands are
dead. Choke. Kick and scream but I ain't got no kick
and all my ears got for me is <u>pantin' pantin' pantin'</u>,
like Sabretooth gone and hidden inside my own head.

It's an oxygen mask say Compo. *Don't worry...* He
look at Mum, like his eyes got somethin' to say to her,
and she strokin' my head and sayin' *We'll get you
safe, we'll get you safe...*

Pantin' slowin' down, calmin' into smooth, deep
breathin', and I'm hearin' sirens.

We in the back of a meat wagon, and I am in need
of sirens. Sirens mean they think I am not dead.
Sirens mean I ain't yet Soft Stuart.

<u>Nee-naw nee-naw.</u> Can you hear 'em?

No more bugs. Con-Con sittin' there, cryin', tears
rollin' down. Don't cry, bro. Don't cry...

I wake up in a bed. I am in a hospital. I have
tubes attached to me. I clench my fists and I feel

my fingers work.

I turn my head and the bedsheets are white, and crisp and clean. There are no bedbugs. A nurse smiles at me. I am smellin' bleach and it is the smell of the Garden of Heaven.

Marsh?

Turn my head round the other way and there is Mum and Connor sittin' there, smilin' and cryin', like they can't make up their minds. I smile back. My mind ain't so indecisive.

You're safe says Mum. Con-Con don't say nothin', jus' sittin' still but I can see by his eyes that inside he bouncin' off the ceilin'.

I look at the ceilin'. It is clear, white. No bugs. I 'member. Everybody believed me. Sis killed all of them bugs. Mum killed the bugs. Compo did. Big Auntie.

My mouth starts movin'. I can move again. I can move. *I was s'posed to save you. I fell asleep. I was little ol' Sleepy Lady. I was dopey ol' Muskrat. Soft. Fell asleep on my watch and let everybody else do my battlin'.*

It's OK says Mum. I guess it is. She squeezin' my fingers. My fingers can feel her fingers. We ain't ballin' our fists, jus' holdin' hands, breathin'. Bein' alive.

Sis?

Sis is fine say Mum. *And Mustapha. Ambulance men called the police. Everybody got out. The Finger is evacuated.*

Tonight?

*It's tomorrow now, Marshy. Everybody is safe.
What's left of those monsters, the army are dealing
with right now.*

I'm thinkin' about this for a minute. *The army?*

Finishing off what we started says Mum. *Sort out
the big ones first. Then the council are going to get
the little ones.*

Proper this time?

Proper.

No more little bugs crawlin' outta my shirt
sleeves. No more bug-poo full stops.

Thinkin' about this. Sleepy...

I wake and Sis and Mus are sittin' by my bed and
they wearin' gowns and they got tubes stickin' outta
their arms and I blink and I say *What? The bugs got
you also?*

No Sis laugh. *You got us, ain't you?*

Huh?

*How you think you got 'nuff blood back dancin'
through your skinny arms?*

Muskrat grin. *Now a part of you will always be me.
Think about it.*

We your blood donors add Sis. *Ain't we kind? We
replace all that the bugs stole.*

Mus start to joke about how I slept through all the
battlin', how even on crutches he could conquer the
Megas, and Sis was a deadly aim.

You missed all the fun, Mallow say Mus.

Look at him, though, ain't he all blissed out now?
<u>Blissed out.</u>
All of a sudden I remember. Try and bolt upright.
Where's Mum? I say.
She in the canteen.
Go get her. Get her now!

Mum arrive back at my bedside and she can see
somethin' is wrong. I take her hand.
I'm sorry, Mum I say.
No. You did good.
No. I am sorry. I hesitate. Only one way to say it. *I
saw Dad.*
Oh. She tries not to look hurt.
*You were right, Mum. It wasn't really my dad, not
like I remember. <u>My</u> dad.*
I'm so sorry. I see she got a tear tricklin' down
her cheek.
It's OK I whisper. *We don' need him, we don'
need him...*
She sit holdin' my hand for a while, and I try to
find the words I need.
I ask *Mum, how many letters did he send?*
There are now no more lies between us.
Not many. A handful. Would you like to see them?
Nor no more distrust.
No. I saw him.
Is he...?
He is no good.

Oh, Marshy... Mum smiles, all sad, puts her hand on my cheek. *You know* she say, *when I heard ... when I heard – that he'd killed a man* – she strokes my face, soft, small – *it almost broke me.*

A strand of hair falls across her face. She is still beautiful.

But it was OK she says. She swallows a sob. *I always had you.*

I smile now. I imagine my smile is sad also. I got one more duty to do. One final duty.

Mum I say, *we got to go back to The Finger. We got to get Compo, and go back...*

It take a bit of persuadin', but here we be, ridin' back to The Finger in a police car, me and Mum and Compo and Inspector Morse.

I am still feeble and my head is all fuzzy I think the hospital got me all drugged up which I think is what they call a <u>irony</u>.

We pull up outside The Finger and it is not the place I remember. We seein' council workmen doin' a clean-up, like the aftermath of a riot. They literally sweepin' dead Megas off the floor like crisp, golden autumn leaves. A pleasure to behold. Cleaners is in, squirtin' down all the walls. Riot vans parked in a huddle all round the car park. Soldiers with rifles and gas masks goin' in and out through the entrance. Place finally gettin' the fumigation it needs.

Where's all the citizens? I ask.

Mum smile sideways at me, sneaky. *Nobody is going back. Can they fumigate the damp sinking down from the roof? Put in a whole new lift? Get the stink out of the busted rubbish chutes? The Finger has been declared unfit. That's unfit for human habitation. We've got a right to live somewhere civilized.*

Compo step up ask me a question. He ain't sure how he should be addressin' me now I am the hero of the hour. Suppose me and him declared a uneasy truce. Either way, it feel right he get to do what he always wanted: clear the last druggie out of his policin' patch.

My dad is dead to me. Even so, I'm hopin' we ain't too late. So I give Comp directions, and he and Morse step inside, and begin their slow walk up them twenty flights.

We wait.

I fixed for Con-Con to be waitin' by the park with Big Auntie. Don' want him to see whatever it is Comp is goin' to carry down. I text Sis and double-check. They all there, Mus and Sabes too.

We wait.

We watch the council cleaners and the army and the firefighters even, and out the corner of my eye I see a TV crew. Now they want to know about the people of The Finger.

We wait.

The doors open. Compo got my dad over his shoulder, fireman's lift. It look like Dad is the littl'un now, and Compo is the dad. Compo is stronger than I thought, twenty floors he carry the weight of my father down. He stride to the meat wagon like he got determination in his legs.

Compo and Morse lift Dad into the back of the ambulance, doors slam shut behind him, like curtain goin' down at the end of a performance. Wagon begin to drive away. I wait, listen out, see whether they have need of the sirens.

Do I care?

<u>I will never be like him.</u>

As the meat wagon drive away, the sirens begin. I am glad.

Minute later, my hound come boundin' up to me, leapin' all over, lickin' me like he thought he'd never see me again. Con-Con come boundin' behind him, also lookin' like he want to lick me all over.

I turn to Mum. *So what happen now?*

Connor is tryin' to reach his arm up, reach his hand onto my shoulder, like we the same height, same age. So I let my hand rest on his shoulder.

You saved a load of lives she says, *my Little Prince.*

How many years since she call me that? Too many.

A lot of people are very grateful, including the council. She can't hold back an excited smile. *We're going to get rehoused.*

When? I say.

Soon enough.

I'm thinkin' about that. What we goin' to do in the meantime?

Mum read my mind. *Big Auntie reckons if we play our cards right, we got to go somewhere, and maybe the council is going to show some genuine gratitude. She's been having a word. Maybe we'll finally get to go on that holiday we always wanted.*

Oh, a rest. A lie-down, without no itchy and scratchy. Beaches. Blue sea. Costa del Whatever.

I stand there, imaginin' it. Aroun' me is laughter and yippin', from my mum and my bro and my dog, and from Sis and Mus and Big Auntie.

My crew.

That sounds fine to me.

I close my eyes, and I take a deep breath.

About the Author

Steve Tasane is a writer and performance poet. He has been writer-in-residence at the V&A Museum of Childhood, Battersea Dogs Home and the Dickens Bicentennial Celebrations, as well as performing at Glastonbury, and on TV and radio. He is a passionate advocate of popular poetry, mentoring young poets and visiting schools to introduce children of every age to his blend of Slam, Rap and Punk.

Steve's poetry and stories have been widely published in anthologies, including How to Be a Boy, and also a solo collection, Bleeding Heart. He was shortlisted for the Diverse Voices Award for Fly Kids. *Everything I've learned in life, about people and animals and love and hate, goes into what I write* he says.

For more about Blood Donors, and extras including The Marshall Chronicles, visit stevetasane. wordpress.com. Find Steve's performance poetry on YouTube or at stevetasane.com.